CIRCLE C CARRIES ON

Center Point
Large Print

Also by Brett Rider and available from Center Point Large Print:

Circle C Moves In

CIRCLE C CARRIES ON

Brett Rider

CENTER POINT LARGE PRINT
THORNDIKE, MAINE

This Center Point Large Print edition
is published in the year 2023 by arrangement with
Golden West Inc.

Originally published in the US by Macrae
Smith Company.

The text of this Large Print edition is unabridged.
In other aspects, this book may vary
from the original edition.
Printed in the United States of America
on permanent paper sourced using
environmentally responsible foresting methods.
Set in 16-point Times New Roman type.

ISBN 978-1-63808-904-9 (hardcover)
ISBN 978-1-63808-908-7 (paperback)

The Library of Congress has cataloged this record
under Library of Congress Control Number: 2023940532

TO OUR FOREBEARS

"A good name is rather to be chosen than great riches."—*Proverbs*

CIRCLE C CARRIES ON

1

The rugged slopes of the Comanches lay dark and forbidding under swift-moving clouds that piled above the higher peaks, drew an obscuring veil across the face of the morning sun. The signs were familiar to young Donal Cameron—the vagrant puffs of wind, the ominous mutterings of thunder. He was in for a pelting rain. The thought cheered his cowman's heart. Rain would literally be manna from the skies to the thirsting range.

There was need for cheer in him. Lonesomeness, a mounting dread put a droop to his shoulders. It was not that he was a stranger here. The trail was familiar enough. He had traveled it more times than memory could recall. This was his own country; another hour would put him on Circle C range, within sight of the sprawling old ranch house where he had been born.

Donal drew his horse to a standstill. He must think this thing out, find the right words. He was not sure that his mother yet knew that he was returning home to Circle C—alone.

Thunder drummed in the hills, drew startled snorts from the horse. Donal came out of his brooding and reached for his slicker, warned by a splash on his face. He had one arm thrust in a sleeve when he heard the voice.

"Hold it, mister," the voice said. "Don't argue . . . just keep as you are."

It was a quiet voice, touched with malicious laughter. Donal stiffened, sent his gaze in a javelin thrust at the shadowed speaker crouching above the trail. He saw a face, a vague blur behind a clump of buckthorn already beaded with raindrops, and he could see the man's eyes, cold, leaden points, sighting along the wet barrel of a rifle.

Brush crackled underfoot, and Donal, not removing his gaze from the man behind the rifle, was uncomfortably aware of other men approaching from below the trail. He forced himself to speak nonchalantly.

"What's the idea? You fellers the law?"

A guffaw answered him. He spoke again. "I reckon there's some mistake here," he said. "If you fellers don't object I'll get this slicker pulled on. Rain's gettin' worse every moment."

Apparently there was no objection. He shrugged into the slicker, disturbingly conscious of hard, scrutinizing eyes, and conscious, too, of a growing anger in him. He said resentfully, "Well—now that you've looked me over I'll be on my way."

The rifle waggled menacingly. "I reckon not," answered the man whose eyes gleamed down the barrel.

"There's some mistake here," Donal repeated.

The man holding the leveled rifle interrupted brusquely. “You’re Don Cameron, ain’t you?”

“That’s my name,” admitted Donal with a brittle laugh. “Donal Cameron of Circle C. And no damn business of yours.”

“You’re awful wrong,” answered the man. “Keep your hands in plain sight, young feller. We’re takin’ that gun before you get notions.”

Donal felt a hand come up from behind and ease the gun from his belt. He offered no resistance, sat rigid in his saddle. The smell of sudden death was in his nostrils.

“Rope him up good, fellers. If he’s like his dad, he’s dynamite.” The man laughed gratingly.

His hitherto unseen companions pressed close on either side of Donal. His hands were seized, drawn down to saddle horn and made fast, and tough rawhide thongs lashed his feet to the stirrups.

The man with the rifle pushed into view from behind the dripping buckthorn. He was tall, and thin, with a squat snub of a nose set in a dark, bony face. The flaring nostrils, the tight-drawn skin, the lips pulled back from long brown teeth in a sinister grimace, gave Donal the unpleasant impression of a death’s head.

“So you’re the Cameron kid, huh?” The grin widened. “Wasn’t sure which one of you was headed back from Cuba.”

Donal only looked at him, anger mixed with

anguish in his eyes, and complete bewilderment. He had never seen this man before, nor the pair in watchful attention on either side of his horse.

"Heard one of you was killed at San Juan Hill," the man went on. "You and your dad wears the same handle to your names, so we wasn't sure which of you was headed back."

"You said that before." Donal spoke huskily. "It's none of your business. I don't know you."

"Your dad would have knowed me," chortled the man. He spat from the side of his mouth, drew the back of a hairy hand across wet lips. "So your dad got himself killed. His own fault for joinin' up with Teddy's Rough Riders. Don Cameron was always a fightin' fool. Reckon you're some like him. Had to go along with them Rough Riders too, huh?"

"What do you want with me?" Donal kept his voice steady. "You've got me guessing."

"You're the boss of Circle C—now your dad is dead," the man said. "That's why we want you."

"I'm still guessing." Donal glowered at his bound wrists. "No savvy this business."

The three men exchanged unpleasant grins, and there was a long silence, broken by one of the tall man's companions.

"No sense takin' him to the ranch, Al." His look went suggestively to the scraggy branch of a piñon tree. "I'll git my rope."

The other man shook his head. "I'm runnin' this show, Ben," he retorted. "We ain't danglin' him so quick. Spoil the play."

Ben scowled. He was a moon-faced chunky man with a slit of a mouth and bulging pale blue eyes. "No sense wastin' time with him," he argued. "He's Don Cameron, ain't he?"

Gober ignored the protest. "Go fetch the broncs," he said to the other man. He grinned at the prisoner. "Ben Ferrel is awful impatient. You wouldn't think it to look at him."

The horses were brought up and the three men climbed into their saddles. Gober headed the procession, with Donal's horse on a lead-rope. Rain dripped steadily, formed rivulets and pools in the trail.

No words came from the men. They rode in a silence touched only by the hissing rain, the splash of hoofs, the jingle of bit and spur. Donal made no attempt to break the silence. He knew that further words would bring no solution to the mystery. He was coming out of his daze. The shock of it had numbed him at first, but his wits were functioning again, his mind coldly analyzing the purpose of these men who had so strangely waylaid him.

He was uncomfortably aware that it was a sinister purpose, something to do with Circle C, and that his life was in deadly peril. Worse still, trouble at Circle C meant trouble for his mother.

The thought sent a chill through him. His senses reeled.

With an effort he steadied himself, fought off the paralyzing fear. It was going to be up to him. He could not afford to let fear cloud his mind. It was not the first time a Cameron of Circle C had faced death with the odds against him.

He forced his mind back to the ranch, to his mother, to Rusty Cross. Rusty was a tower of strength, a reassuring thought at that moment. Rusty had been foreman ever since the time Circle C had come up from the Brazos and taken root in the Rio Seco country. A small outfit in those days, but one that had made cow history. Old-timers still talked of how Donal Cameron had moved in on Jim Daker's hitherto undisputed domain and held it despite hell and high water. The story was a saga of grim courage, a legend that grew with the years, and the man who had given his life for his country at San Juan Hill was the beating heart of that legend.

Courage quickened in him as he thought of his father. He had the feeling that his father was very close, siding him in this desperate hour, whispering words in his ear, counseling him from his vast store of experience. This was a time for cool thinking, for lightning action when the moment was ripe. It was up to him to seize the one chance when it came. There was always that one chance for the man who was primed and ready.

He glanced over his shoulder, met a mirthless grin from Ben Ferrel. For all his moon face, there was a formidable look to the man. His slit of a mouth, his staring marble eyes, made Donal think of a shark. He was quite as dangerous as the tall leader with the death's-head face.

Donal's quick look reached to the man bringing up the rear. A lumpish, stupid face under a Mexican steeple hat. There was mixed blood in him, and all of it bad.

The trail plunged down a steep slope. Donal's gaze probed through the slanting rain. He remembered this narrow gorge. It angled into Aliso Creek Canyon where the trail would presently fork. The south turn led to the old Daker ranch house while the main trail continued up the canyon to the ridge route into the town of San Benito.

He ventured a question. "Heading for town?" he called to the rider in front of him.

Gober turned his head in a brief look back at him. "I'm headin' there," he answered. "*You* ain't."

Donal's eyes narrowed in a hard look at the long, gaunt back of the man. There was a chilling implication in his terse answer. They were going to kill him, leave his body in the chaparral for the buzzards.

With an effort he checked the frantic impulse to strain at the thongs that bound his hands to the saddle horn. No sense in wasting his strength.

The thongs were tough, and the knots tied by men who knew their business. He fought off, too, the numbing clutch of despair. He must continue to hope, keep himself ready for the one chance when it came.

Gober halted his horse in the fork of the trail. Ferrel and the man under the steeple hat drew alongside, hard eyes intent on him as he drawled out his instruction.

"I'm headin' for San Benito," he told them. "You an' Squint can make for the ranch with this jasper."

"No sense takin' him to the ranch," Ferrel again protested. "I'm for fixin' him right now."

Gober's face darkened. "Anse won't like it," he said impatiently. "Anse wants this feller alive—until he's done with him." He paused, added significantly, "I'm warnin' you, Ben. Don't you get notions."

Ferrel's moon face took on a greenish look. "I ain't buckin' Anse," he muttered.

"That's better talk," approved Gober. "You take good care of Cameron until I get back from town with Anse." His eyes swung to Donal in a thoughtful look. "Watch him close, fellers. Anse will sure take your skelps if you let him bust loose."

"Bust loose nothin'," sneered Ferrel. He flung a contemptuous glance at the prisoner. "Not with *me* on the job."

Gober grunted, touched spurs to his unwilling horse and moved up the trail, head bent against the driving rain.

With Donal's horse following on a lead-rope, Ferrel pushed into the south fork. Squint trailed them. Donal stared back at him, a quick, searching look that stirred in him a shred of hope. Gober and Ferrel were tough and wary men, hard to outwit, but he sensed a weak link in their stupid-faced companion. It was the weak link he must look for.

He began to speculate about the man Gober had gone to fetch from San Benito. He could not recall anybody named Anse. Apparently he was a newcomer, and the leader, or one of the leaders of this mysterious gang. It was equally obvious that he was a man to be feared, judging from Ferrel's reaction to Gober's warning. Ferrel's moon face had registered sheer terror. The thought was grimly reassuring. The danger would not reach its peak until Gober returned from town with the mysterious Anse. For the moment he was safe from immediate harm. He would have a few precious hours—and he would make the most of them.

The trail swung left into a road that reached through a grove of giant cottonwoods. Donal picked up a rain-blurred view of the Daker ranch house. He was acutely conscious of a shocked disbelief in the familiar scene. The Rocking D had once been like a second home to him. Jim Daker and his father had been firm friends ever since he could remember. The grim old cowman had been "Uncle Jim" to him. He had bulldogged his first calf in Jim Daker's corral. And now he was riding up that winding avenue, a helpless and completely mystified prisoner. He could make neither head nor tail of it. Only one fact stood out, stark and ugly. Jim Daker's Rocking D had fallen into sinister hands since his death. The once friendly ranch was now hostile country.

A man slouched into view, stood waiting at the entrance to the big yard. The glinting metal of a rifle peeped from under the folds of his wet slicker. He peered at them through the rain, a hint of curiosity, and ill-temper, in his eyes.

"What's that you got?" he asked, grumpily.

"What the hell do you think?" retorted Ferrel.

"I figgered Cameron was some older," the man said. "This maverick's only a kid."

"He's Cameron's kid, and that means he's like to be hell on wheels, give him a chance," Ferrel said with a grim smile. "He's Circle C, now his pappy's dead, Alamo."

Alamo turned a coldly-appraising stare on the prisoner. "His looks don't scare me none, Ben." There was a sneer in his drawling voice, but the enigmatic glint in his eyes made Donal wonder.

"Al is headed for town to fetch the boss," Ferrel told him. He scowled. "I was all set for stringin' the pup to a tree, but Al figgered to keep him for Anse." He started his horse through the gate.

Alamo's quick gesture stopped him. "I've been stickin' here sence afore sunup," complained the man. "You send some feller to keep watch at the gate, Ben. I'm cravin' food an' hot coffee."

"Sure," grinned Ferrel. "Can do with a pot of coffee my own self."

"Me too," chortled Squint from under his dripping steeple hat.

Ferrel regarded him with malicious eyes. "You're stickin' with the gate for a while," he said. "You've et breakfast and Alamo ain't."

Squint muttered an angry malediction. Ferrel gave him a mirthless smile. "I'll send a feller to relieve you," he promised. "Just as quick as Alamo and me get this jasper stowed safe in the calaboose." He pushed through the gate, hand jerking the lead-rope of Donal's horse.

Alamo trailed them, long legs bending at the knees in an awkward, shambling gait that carried him along at an amazing speed. Donal's quick backward glance took him in, noted that long, loose-jointed stride. Not the short, choppy walk of a cowman on high bootheels. The deceptively fast pace of a mountain man, accustomed to long journeys on foot through the trackless wilderness. Donal guessed shrewdly that Alamo was not a product of the cattle range, but a hangover from the days of the fur brigade when those hardy, half-wild men ranged remote rivers and creeks in quest of the beaver. Wilderness scouts, that roaring turbulent crew, and makers of trails for the wagons and railroads to follow.

Something else caught his attention in that brief look at the man, the upward flip of his hand in a furtive gesture, palm out-thrust.

Donal stared with unseeing eyes at the big barn that loomed up through the curtain of rain. That guarded gesture was Indian sign-talk, a signal of friendship.

He dared another look. His bound hands prevented a return signal, but he flashed a quick smile, caught an answering grin on Alamo's bearded lips, and again that fleeting out-thrust of open palm.

Ferrel drew to a halt in front of a squat building that stood between two ancient cottonwood trees. Donal recognized the place. When a small boy he had often played inside those stout adobe walls, putting up a desperate defense against imaginary Comanche war parties. There were times when Jim Daker would join him and tell him fascinating tales of old Mangus Colorado and raiding Apaches, when the building had been used as a fort against their attacks.

A man, carrying a pitchfork, hurried from the barn. Another man slammed out of the bunkhouse and ran toward them. Ferrel climbed from his saddle and tossed the lead-rope to Alamo as he shambled up alongside Donal's horse. "I reckon the granary will hold him safe till Al and Anse get here," he grinned at the man with the pitchfork. "Open the door, Calico."

Calico, head craned in a deeply interested look at the prisoner, leaned his pitchfork against the adobe wall and slid the iron bar. The door creaked open to the push of his foot.

At a nod from Ferrel, the man from the bunk-house jerked his gun from holster and stood watching while Alamo untied the ropes. Donal slid from the saddle, and at a gesture from Ferrel went slowly inside.

Ferrel and the others crowded in at his heels, and Ferrel said thoughtfully, "No chance for him to bust loose from here, but I ain't takin' bets he won't try."

"No chance a-tall," asserted Alamo. "Couldn't bust out of here in a million years."

Ferrel shook his head. "Won't take no gamble with him," he said. "Tie him up ag'in, Alamo."

"Sure." Alamo looked at Donal, the rawhide thongs dangling from his hand. "Be some softer if you lay on them grain sacks, young feller."

"*Gracias.*" Donal forced a grin and stretched out on the pile of sacks under a narrow barred window set high in the wall. Alamo bent over him, swiftly re-tied his ankles and wrists.

"Make them knots tight," Ferrel said gruffly.

"Sure," repeated Alamo. He jerked at the ropes,

his bearded face lowered close to the prisoner's. Donal read an unspoken message in the man's deep-set eyes. He kept his own face blank, fearful of Ferrel's watchful gaze.

Alamo straightened up, grinned at his companions. "You can gamble plenty on *them* knots," he said to Ferrel.

The man nodded. "We'll have Calico keep watch on the door," he decided.

Calico gave him a sour look. The rain was beating in under the press of a rising wind. He had no relish for the job. "I'll go git my slicker—and my gun," he said sullenly.

The others followed him outside. The heavy door was pulled shut with a slam. Donal heard the muffled clang of the iron bar, the low murmur of voices, and then the thud and splash of hoofs as the horses were led away to the barn.

2

He lay motionless for long minutes, accustoming his eyes to the deeper shadows that filled the room with the closing of the door. Light filtered dimly through the small barred windows that centered the four walls which were also pierced with loopholes placed shoulder-high. He raised his head and studied the loopholes carefully, saw they had been sealed off from the outside with strips of tin. A necessary precaution against rodents getting into the store of grain. The four windows were similarly protected with coarse wire mesh. They were actually nothing more than unglazed openings to admit light and air.

Reassured to know that he could not be seen by eyes watching at a loophole, he lowered his gaze to the rawhide rope that noosed his wrists and ran down to the thongs that secured his ankles. He could see nothing wrong with that job of tying. Ferrel had apparently been satisfied. It would have been hard for Alamo to fool him. And yet that message in the man's eyes had been plain enough. He had wanted Donal to know that those knots would work loose.

Donal lifted his feet, wiggled them tentatively. The cords held firm. His hopes began to dwindle. He must have misread the look in Alamo's eyes.

He relaxed for a long moment, his thoughts racing. Footsteps approached the building. Calico, returning from the barn with his slicker and gun.

The iron bar slid back with a rusty squeal, the door opened and Donal saw the choreman's face peering in at him. Rain dribbled from his hat, drew dancing gleams from the slicker. He was a scrawny, bow-legged man with an untidy mustache and mean little eyes. Apparently he only wanted to satisfy himself that his prisoner was safe. He withdrew his head and the door swung shut.

The instant he heard the scrape of the bolt sliding back in its socket, Donal ventured another attempt on the ropes. He drew his knees up and holding the position strained at his bound wrists. The result was discouraging. The cords tightened.

Desperate now, he shoved his legs out in a violent downward thrust and felt the ropes suddenly go slack. He tried again, and this time Alamo's cunningly-tied knot slipped free.

He shook off the loose cords and got cautiously to his feet. He felt all the nervous apprehensions of a man set blindfolded on the edge of a precipice. Alamo's extraordinary behavior had him guessing wildly and he had no idea what he was supposed to do now that he had solved the secret of the trick knot. He stood there, irresolute, forcing himself to think the thing out coolly.

One fact loomed big in his confused mind. There must be no blunder, no betraying sound to draw Calico's attention.

His straining ears heard only the muted drumming of the rain on the roof, and it came to him that Calico was probably keeping watch from under the sheltering branches of one of the big cottonwood trees that flanked the granary. The man's interest would be centered on the door, and that only casually. It would not enter his mind that the prisoner could possibly free himself from the ropes that bound him hand and foot.

He turned appraising eyes on the small barred windows. They were little more than slits, too narrow for a man to squeeze through, even if he could wrench out the bars. And the adobe walls were solid enough, his quick search discovered.

He halted near the door and stared around with desperate eyes. There was nothing in the place he could use for a weapon. Only some piles of empty grain sacks—the straw that littered the floor.

Ugly thoughts pressed in on him as he stood there. Alamo had been amusing himself, holding out hopes merely to torture the prisoner. The man had no intention of helping him escape and the incident of the trick knots was only a diabolical joke.

His alert ears picked up the sound of approaching feet slopping through pools of water.

His reaction was instantaneous, a stealthy, lightning move that brought him close to the wall in a position where the opening of the door would cover him from immediate discovery.

The iron bar scraped back with its rusty squeal and the door pushed open. Donal crouched behind it. He was like a great cat waiting for the deadly leap on an unsuspecting victim.

There was a brief silence, a muttered exclamation. Calico stepped inside, astonished gaze fixed on the pile of sacks where his prisoner should have been lying. Too late he realized his danger and reached for his gun. Donal seized the lowered hand in a grip that jerked the man off balance. In another moment Donal had the gun.

He was in no mood for temporizing. He swung the gun barrel with ruthless force against Calico's head. As the senseless man crumpled to the straw Donal turned swiftly to the open door, alarmed by a stealthy movement outside. A shape appeared from the curtain of rain, materialized into the lanky form of Alamo.

Donal lifted the gun, gestured for the man to come inside. Alamo's deep-set eyes flashed him an astonished look as he obeyed.

"Keep your hands up," Donal said in a voice hardly audible above the hissing rain.

Alamo lifted his hands, watched in silence while Donal shut the door with the toe of his boot.

They stared at each other in that same grim silence, Donal's eyes coldly watchful, the older man's filling with a curious warmth. He broke the silence.

"You look like your dad looked one time down on the Brazos," he said softly. "Twenty-five years ago, it was, and I thought for a minute I was seein' him ag'in the same as that night when me and him bust loose from Lobo Jack's bunch of killers." He grinned. "You don't need to keep that gun on me, son," he added mildly.

Donal made no move to lower the menacing gun. "What did you want here?" he asked bluntly.

Alamo's surprise was real. "Shouldn't be hard for you to savvy," he drawled. He flicked a glance at the senseless Calico. "I was figgerin' to finish the job of gittin' you away from this damn place. Seems like you wasn't needin' my help." His grin widened.

Donal lowered the gun. "What were you planning to do?"

"Was in my mind to trick Calico away from the door," Alamo explained. "Fetched a gun along for you." He unfastened a cartridge-filled belt, its holster sagging with the weight of a long-barreled Colt .45.

Donal buckled the belt around his lean hips. His mind was in a whirl, despite his resolve to keep cool. This strange man had once known his father, had fought by his side. He said huskily, "I don't understand, Alamo, but I'm not forgetting."

"I been owin' it to Don Cameron a lot of years," Alamo said simply. "They didn't come better than him, son. He was all *man*." His attention went to the senseless Calico. "We'll tie him up good, and make tracks away from here." He smiled wryly. "Sure will leave plenty tracks with the ground so wet."

They went to work with swift, sure fingers and in a few moments Calico was lying securely trussed on the straw.

"Them knots will stay put *this* time," Alamo said with a sly grin.

Donal stared down at the prone man. "Looks like he's coming out of it," he said. "We don't want him yelling for help."

Alamo jerked a soiled bandanna from Calico's pocket and expertly improvised a gag. "Won't do no yellin' now," he chuckled. "Come on, son. Let's git away from here." He turned to the door.

Donal wasted no time with questions. It was obvious that Alamo knew what he was doing. With a last look at Calico he followed his new-found friend into the pelting rain.

Alamo slid the rusty bar and secured it with the heavy padlock. "We'll drop the key in the crik some place," he said with another chuckle. "Ben Ferrel's goin' to be awful puzzled when he finds the door locked and Calico gone from his post. He'll figure Calico snapped the padlock and went off to the barn to git out of the rain. They'll lose time lookin' for him, and time is what me and you want plenty of."

He moved with his long, shambling stride through a corral gate back of the barn. Donal followed at his heels, eyes alert, gun ready in his hand.

In a few minutes they were lost to view in a dense growth of alders. Alamo said over his shoulder, "Got horses waitin' other side of the crik."

They came to the creek, shallow, and rain-splashed, and showing a boulder-strewn bed. Alamo plunged in with a gesture for Donal to follow, and they waded down-stream for some fifty yards.

Up on the opposite bank, Alamo paused and glanced at his companion. "Our tracks is plain enough, down to the crik. Take 'em a lot of time to pick 'em up ag'in, not knowin' which way we turned." He continued up the bank.

Five minutes brought them to a great over-hanging rock and Donal saw three horses, and, to his growing amazement, a slim youth standing half concealed behind the fringe of bushes. His low ejaculation drew a look from Alamo.

"S'prised, huh?" he drawled. "Waal, she's goin' with us, son. Ain't had time to tell you about her."

They were moving fast, and Donal's second and

closer look told him that the slim shape huddled in the wet slicker was indeed a girl for all her masculine garb. She gave him a brief glance, fixed inquiring brown eyes on Alamo.

"Fork your saddle, Ruth," he said curtly. "We're headin' away from here fast." He gestured at his companion. "Don wasn't waitin'. Had Calico laid out cold and was all set to bust out on his own."

The girl flashed Donal a curious look and turned quickly to the horses. In another moment the three were in their saddles and riding up the slope.

Alamo took the lead and Donal found his big roan horse alongside the girl's trim chestnut mare. Her head lifted in a sidewise look at him, and he caught a glimpse of warm, dark eyes under the wide brim of her dripping hat. She looked young, perhaps in her late 'teens, and he sensed fear in her, from the paleness that marked her face, the tightened lips. There was courage, though, in every line of her. He said quietly, "I don't know what it's all about. Do you?"

She gave him another quick look, and he saw surprise in her eyes, a hint of doubt. "*You* should know, that is if you really are Don Cameron."

It was the first time he had heard her voice. He liked the sound of it, and he liked the forthright manner of her.

"That's my name—" He paused, added drily,

"I've been away from this country for over a year. Don't remember seeing you before."

"You wouldn't," she said. "I've only been here a few months."

"And now you seem to be running away," Donal said a bit grimly.

She kept her eyes on the tall, gangling rider in front of them, and there was no answer from her.

Donal rode on in silence for a time, his mind wrestling with vague memories. Old Jim Daker had let words drop, something about a nephew in New Orleans. He had married a girl there. The name came to him suddenly and he swept his companion with a comprehensive look in which there appeared a gleam of excitement.

"You're Colonel Tony Merrill's daughter," he said, "and that makes Jim Daker your great-uncle."

"Yes," she admitted, not looking at him.

"Jim Daker left the ranch to Colonel Merrill, didn't he?"

"Yes," she said again. Her dark eyes met his and he saw hardness in their depths.

He stared at her, a frown in his own eyes. "Why are you running away?"

"Because I'm frightened," she told him simply.

The slope steepened, forced the horses to scramble, and their shod hoofs dislodged little avalanches of loose stones that went rattling down into the gorge. Rain-sodden branches clawed at them and the girl's chestnut mare began to show signs of panic. Donal grabbed at her bridle in time to keep her from swerving down the hill.

"I can manage," the girl said. "You needn't hold her."

He grinned, relinquishing his grasp.

The incident had put color into her cheeks, cleared the fear from her eyes. Donal was aware of a curious warmth in him as he looked at her. She was different from any girl he had ever known.

They drew alongside Alamo, waiting for them on the summit. "Won't be so tough, now we've cut the trail," he said. His approving smile touched the girl. "You've sure got plenty nerve. Thar's folks wouldn't want to face that hill."

"I was frightened stiff," Ruth Merrill confessed.

"Git a slide started and thar's hell to pay," Alamo said. He smiled at her. "At that, stayin' at the ranch would have been a heap worse."

"Yes." Her face paled. "A lot worse."

Donal was studying the landscape. "This trail heads down to Tule Flats," he said.

"Sure," agreed Alamo laconically.

"Circle C lies over there."

"That's whar you aim to git to, ain't it?" chuckled Alamo. He paused, said a bit grimly, "If you ain't objectin', son, me and Ruth will ride along with you to Circle C. We kind of burned our bridges back at Rocking D. Hell's due to bust loose when Al Gober gits in with Anse Jasey."

Donal said simply, "Let's ride—"

Alamo took the lead again. It was a narrow trail and they were forced to proceed in single file, the girl behind Alamo. Donal's roan followed close on the chestnut's heels.

A rift in the blanketing clouds showed a ragged patch of blue sky. The rain slackened, turned into a mist, and suddenly the sun broke through and the mist was gone.

The rush of bright sunlight quickened Donal's spirits. They were on the west slope of the Comanches, and far below he could see the silver thread of Tule Creek where it snaked across the flats to join the Rio Seco.

He found himself wondering about the girl in front of him, the reason for her flight from the ranch her father had inherited from old Jim Daker. It was obvious that Circle C was involved in the same dangerous intrigue that menaced Rocking D, and that a man known as Anse Jasey was the mainspring of the plot.

Donal's eyes narrowed worriedly. They would soon be out of the gorge and on the ridge where the trail intersected the San Benito road. The chances were even they would run into Al Gober and Jasey on their way from town. For the girl's sake they must avoid so dangerous an encounter.

It seemed that the same thought was in Alamo's

mind. He halted the horses, hand lifted in a gesture for the others to join him.

"San Benito road ahead," he said. "Ain't wanting for us to run smack into Gober and Jasey. Likely have a bunch of fellers with 'em."

Donal nodded. "You wait here with Miss Merrill," he suggested. "I'll ride up to the fork and have a look."

"I'll do the scoutin'," demurred Alamo. His deep-set eyes twinkled. "Was scoutin' Injuns afore you was born, son." He slid from the saddle and took his long-barreled Sharps rifle from its leather sheath. "I reckon you'd best pull off the trail," he added with a backward glance at Donal. In another moment he was lost to view in the brush.

Donal reached for the dangling reins of Alamo's horse and pushed down the slope to a sprawling clump of piñons. Ruth followed him, drew alongside behind the low covered branches. She gave him a rueful little smile.

"I'm afraid I'm an awful nuisance," she said. "You wouldn't be so careful if I were not along." She touched the .32 in her belt. "I know how to shoot a gun. You needn't baby me."

"We don't want any shooting—yet," Donal told her with a grin. His face sobered. "We've been moving so fast there's been no time for questions. I'm asking a few while we wait here for Alamo."

"Hasn't Alamo told you *anything?*" Her surprise was genuine.

He shook his head. "I said there's been no time. I can only guess at things." He paused, then abruptly, "Where is Colonel Merrill?"

Ruth looked at him a long moment, and the misery he read in her dark eyes sent a chill through him. He spoke quickly, compassionately. "You mean he is—dead?"

She nodded. "He—he was murdered—"

Donal looked at her with shocked eyes. Old Jim Daker's nephew dead—murdered—and his daughter now on the run for her life. He said awkwardly, "I didn't know. I'm terribly sorry. When did it happen?"

"Last week—" Her voice hardened. "They tried to make me believe it was an accident—but it was murder. They killed him."

"You have proof?" asked Donal.

She frowned. "Need you ask—after what they did to you? They were going to—to kill you, too."

He recognized the logic, nodded grimly. The girl studied him curiously. His face had taken on a stern, set look that made him seem older than his years. There was strength in his long, lean body, and quiet efficiency in his steady eyes. She sensed unwavering courage in him, a resoluteness that for some reason she found reassuring—comforting.

A rustle in the bushes drew their eyes and they saw Alamo approaching. For all his shambling stride, he moved with amazing lightness. He halted, long rifle in lowered hand, and fished a piece of tobacco from a pocket. "They ain't passed the fork yet," he told his companions. He gnawed off a chew and replaced the tobacco.

"How can you tell?" inquired Ruth.

"Would have been plenty tracks with the ground so wet," answered Alamo. He wagged his bearded face. "One trouble with the ground bein' wet we cain't pick up their dust sign. The road's so doggone crooked, no chance to see 'em comin'." His tone was doubtful. "Would sure hate for 'em to come along just when we hit the road."

Ruth saw their indecision. "I don't want to wait down here," she said quickly. "They might not come for hours."

The two men exchanged looks, and Donal said reluctantly, "She's right, Alamo."

The older man nodded agreement. He swung up to his saddle and without more words they headed back into the trail.

Fifteen minutes brought them to the narrow road that twisted through the piñons. They turned west toward town, splashing through innumerable pools of water that filled the chuckholes. Donal explained to the girl that it was necessary to follow the wagon road for nearly a quarter of a mile before they picked up the trail on the south slope. There was no other way for a rider to penetrate the brush-choked hillside. A man on foot could work his way down, but a horseman had to stick to the trail or invite disaster.

They rode cautiously, Alamo in the lead, long gaunt body hunched forward, his eyes alert on the road twisting darkly between the rain-drenched piñons. Each succeeding sharp bend might bring them face to face with the men they wished to avoid. The soft mud smothered sound and there were no betraying dust drifts to warn them of approaching horsemen.

Their horses moving at a fast shuffling walk they reached the last bend between them and the trail they sought. Almost at the same instant a lone horseman rode into view from the next turn some three hundred yards distant. He halted, yelled back at unseen companions. Three more riders swung into the turn, followed by a buckboard in which sat two men.

Donal said to the girl, “Keep moving.” He gestured at the trail, now less than twenty yards away, and spurred alongside Alamo who was reaching for his long rifle.

It was evident they had been recognized. Loud yells floated up, and riders and buckboard surged into motion.

Donal looked back at Ruth, saw that she was sending the chestnut mare down the trail.

Alamo was sighting along the barrel of his Sharps.

Even as the long rifle roared, Donal flung two quick shots. The distance was too great for his .45, but it spoke a language those oncoming men would understand.

The distance was no handicap for Alamo's big single-shot rifle. The bone-smashing bullet sent one of the riders tumbling from his saddle and his frightened horse wheeled sharply and collided with the buckboard team. Donal heard the rending crash of wood as the buckboard overturned. The other riders swerved their horses into the covering piñons.

"Ain't likin' the way we talk to 'em," chuckled Alamo. He was hastily reloading his rifle.

"Let's get away from here," Donal urged. He was watching the two men unscramble themselves from the wrecked buckboard. One of them was the unmistakable Al Gober and it was apparent that he had incurred some damage. He lowered himself to a fallen log and began to rub his head. The other man was uninjured, judging from the speed he showed in making for the concealment of a bush.

"Anse Jasey," Alamo told Donal, "and pizen mean. I'd sure like to git my Sharps lined up good on him."

"Let's get away from here," repeated Donal. "We've got them stopped for the moment."

"I'll say we got 'em stopped," grinned Alamo. "You're talkin' good sense at that, son," he added grimly. "Be a right smart idee for us to light out afore they git organized for action. Anse Jasey ain't the kind you can take chances with."

They found Ruth waiting a few yards down-trail. Donal met her questioning look with a reassuring nod. "Alamo's shot scared the team," he told her. "Smashed the buckboard. They've had enough of us for this time." He saw no reason to tell her that a man had been killed.

She smiled faintly. "I heard the crash," was all she said.

Alamo grinned at her complacently. "Al Gober is settin' on a log, rubbin' his head. Looks like he got bumped some rough, doggone his ornery hide."

"He frightens me," Ruth said in a low voice. "He looks like a death's head." She repressed a shiver.

Donal glanced at her sharply, puzzled at her sudden paleness, and wondering if she suspected that Al Gober was the murderer of her father.

3

Marica Torres paused in the doorway of the kitchen and spoke in Spanish over her shoulder to the stout Mexican woman who stood at the big brick range, eyes intent on a gently simmering pot. "Bring the broth the moment it is ready, Rafaela." She gestured tragically. "Ah, I grieve so much for our dear señora."

"It is indeed most dreadful for her—for all of us," responded the cook. "First the good señor, to die so far away from us, and now it is our Señor Cross, so foully shot in the back—*murdered.*" She crossed herself swiftly. "*Madre de Dios*! What are we to do—and the young señor nobody knows where."

"There is Pasqual," Marica Torres said with the proud little lift of her head that was hers whenever she spoke of her son. "His grandfather and his grandfather's father were both chief of vaqueros in the old days when Don Fidel was master here."

"*Si*," agreed Rafaela. "There is Pasqual. He knows this *rancho* as he knows the palm of his hand."

Marica Torres let the screen door swing shut and moved slowly along the *galeria* with the graceful step of her race. She was a woman in the early fifties and inclined now to plumpness. Her smooth hair, though, still had the sheen of a raven's wing and there was luster in the fine dark eyes now shadowed with distress.

A grizzled-haired man pushed through the patio gate. A rifle dangled from one hand and two long-barreled Colts swung in holsters at either hip. Catching sight of Marica he hurried up the flagstoned path and intercepted her near the open door of the big hall.

"How's she doin', Marica?" His voice was sharp with anxiety. "My Gawd, I'm about crazy—"

The Mexican woman shook her head. "She mooch un'appy for no 'ave word from young señor, and she sad for poor Señor Cross."

"It's hell," groaned the cowboy. "Ol' Bear-cat's fit to be tied, what with the boss killed over to Cuba, an' now Rusty gittin' a damn bush-whacker's hot lead in his back." He pushed his big hat to the back of his head and agitatedly rubbed his hair. "Wish ol' Sinful wasn't layin' in his grave, an' Rubio an' Wes Coles. Them three fightin' fools would sure be rarin' to go git the skelp of the damn coyote that killed Rusty Cross."

Marica gestured hopelessly. "*Ay Dios mio*," she sighed. "I 'ave live on thees *rancho* w'en Don Fidel Salazar 'ere. I 'ave seen mooch bad theengs 'appen on thees *rancho*—like w'en *los Indios* come." She crossed herself. "My leetle *madre*—she keeled that time weeth all of them."

Memories that hurt put a scowl on Brasca's weathered face, memories that went back more than a score of years, to the time when Circle C had come up from the Brazos and moved in on the old *rancho* Donal Cameron had purchased from the last living heir of the murdered Don Fidel Salazar. Only Bearcat and himself remained of the tough and hardy outfit that had put the fear of God and Circle C into the lawless heart of the Rio Seco country.

He swore fervently, heedless of Marica's shocked face. "My Gawd—it's sure tough on Isabel. Sure wish the kid would show up!"

The housekeeper put fingers to lips. "Too mooch loud you talk. She will 'ear you—" Marica broke off with a startled exclamation and turned embarrassed eyes on the slimly erect woman standing in the doorway. "Señora!" Her tone was a mixture of reproof and dismay. "You mus' no leave your bed so queek. You 'ave the beeg shock."

"I'm all right—" There was no hint of hysteria in Isabel Cameron's cool, low voice. Her look went to Brasca. "Any clues—yet?"

The cowboy shook his head gloomily. "The feller that done it must have been wearin' spook's feet," he said. "Cain't pick up sign on him no place. Bearcat is out with Pasqual now, combin' the tule swamp other side of the crik."

"They won't find him," Mrs. Cameron prophesied.

"Sure we'll find him," asserted Brasca. "No damn cow thief is goin' to bushwhack Rusty Cross an' git away with it. We'll ketch him an' dangle him from the nearest tree."

Mrs. Cameron shook her head. "It's not the work of a cow thief," she said quietly. "This thing goes deeper than that, Brasca." She hesitated. "You see, I have reason to know."

Brasca eyed her worriedly. He said gruffly, "I reckon I don't savvy, ma'am."

Marica again intruded with her protests. "Please, señora, you lie down queek," she implored. "Rafaela breeng 'ot broth for you—"

"I'm all right," repeated Mrs. Cameron. She moved to a bench in the *galeria*. "I'll be glad for the broth," she added, and took the cup from the tray the cook brought to her.

Brasca said awkwardly, "I'll git back to the gate—"

"You can keep an eye on the gate from here," Mrs. Cameron said. She patted the bench. "Sit down by me." Her faint smile touched the Winchester in his hand. "It's comforting to have you and your guns so close." Her fond look was on him. "You are a fast man with a gun, Brasca, even after all these years."

"The boss was faster," Brasca said. He averted his eyes, fearing to betray his emotion.

"Yes," Isabel Cameron spoke softly. "There was nobody like—like the boss." She looked at the trees, their wet branches aglitter with countless dew drops. "A good rain, Brasca," she said. "We were needing a real rain."

Brasca ignored the remark. He said almost challengingly, "The kid's certainly the spittin' image of him."

Her eyes warmed, and she turned and looked at him. "You really think so, Brasca?"

"He's the boss over ag'in," declared the cowboy. "Looks like him, talks like him an' has all the cold nerve an' savvy the boss ever had."

"Thank you," Mrs. Cameron said.

"Mebbe some short on cow savvy," Brasca added honestly. "Him bein' off at collidge an' goin' with them Rough Riders and the boss." The veteran Circle C man rubbed a stubbly chin reflectively. "I reckon me an' Bearcat can take the slack out of *that* rope," he finished.

Mrs. Cameron looked at him with a faint smile. "What you and Bearcat don't know about cows isn't worth knowing," she agreed.

Marica Torres, an interested listener, said with a show of annoyance, "You mus' no forget my Pasqual. All 'ees life 'e ride weeth the cow. My Pasqual 'ees *grande vaquero.*"

"Sure," grinned Brasca. "They don't come better than Pasqual. He's Circle C—same as Bearcat an' me." He was suddenly on his feet, alert eyes fixed on the gate. "Horses!" he exclaimed, and ran with clattering bootheels down the flagstones.

Isabel Cameron sprang from the bench, a hand reaching to the startled housekeeper, her gaze fixed on the riders whose faces were barely visible above the patio gate. "Marica—it's—it's Don—my son—come home at last!" The words tore from her throat in a painful gasp, and suddenly she was running down the steps. The jeweled drops glittering in the trees were not more bright than her eyes.

Marica's hand went to her heart, the quick tears in her fine eyes. It was indeed he riding into the yard—young Don Cameron—and he was not alone. A girl rode by his side, and a great tall man bearded like a prophet of old. Marica's wonder and curiosity put wings to her feet.

Donal saw his mother coming through the gate. He dropped down from his saddle and ran to meet her and drew her into a tight hug. Words came from them, incoherent words that made a melody of happiness. She pushed him away from her, held him at arms' length, hands on his shoulders, and looked him over carefully, her eyes bright with joy, and yet oddly appraising.

"You've grown up," she said. She spoke huskily. "You are more than ever like your father." Her eyes filled. "Donal, my son, trouble has come to Circle C. It will take all that same unfaltering courage that was his, all his coolness—his wisdom if we are to save Circle C."

His silence as he looked at her, the hard lines that grooved his stern young face, carried a message that seemed to strike at her heart. She recoiled, her face pale, horror in her dark eyes.

"Donal! You mean—"

"Yes," he said, and the steel in his voice made her wince for the sharp memory it brought of the other Donal Cameron.

She forced herself to speak calmly. "You must tell me about it." Her look went to the girl, and the grizzled-bearded man, still on their horses and watching this meeting between mother and son. "I must meet your friends, Donal."

"She's Colonel Merrill's daughter," Donal explained. "There's trouble at Rocking D and she had to leave in a hurry." He hesitated. "Alamo got me out of a jam and so I had him and Ruth Merrill come along with me."

Mrs. Cameron was already moving swiftly to the slim, tired-faced girl sitting so erect in her saddle. "I'm so glad you've come."

Ruth slid from her saddle. Mrs. Cameron slipped a comforting arm around her and turned a smile on Alamo as he swung to the ground. "Circle C welcomes any friend of Donal's," she said to him.

"Waal—" Alamo grinned at her. "As for that, I knowed his dad back in the old days on the Brazos." He extended a huge, hairy hand. "Alamo Jones is the name, ma'am, and mighty proud to meet you."

Isabel Cameron stared at him, recollection dawning in her eyes. "Alamo Jones! Why—why my husband used to speak of you so often. He—he—" Her voice choked and she could only smile at him with eyes that held a hint of tears.

"Sure, sure," rumbled Alamo. His big hand patted her gently on the shoulder. "He ain't here no more, but he's left a boy that'll play the hand out, an' play it the way he would."

Isabel Cameron's eyes thanked him. She turned to the girl. "Come with me, Ruth. You look so tired, my dear." Her eyes took in the torn, wet clothes. "You've had a hard ride."

"I didn't mind," Ruth said. "Anything was better than—than staying there—after what happened."

The anguish in her low voice drew another keen look from the older woman. Her eyes questioned Donal, read the truth in the hard set of his face.

"Colonel Merrill is dead," he told her. "Murdered—"

She gazed at him, too shocked for words, tightened her arm about the girl's waist.

Brasca broke the brief silence. He said in a harsh voice, "Looks like you're right, ma'am. Hell's sure bust loose in Rio Seco."

Donal's gaze turned to him in a long, hard look.

He had known the grizzled cowboy all his life and sensed there was more to come. A chill went through him as he saw the pain, the reluctance in the man's eyes.

He heard his mother's voice, touched with heartfelt grief. "It's bad news, Donal, about Rusty. He was killed last night—shot in the back."

Donal could only look at her. Rusty Cross dead—murdered. Good old Rusty, one of the faithful crew that had come up from the Brazos with his father, and who for more than a score of years had bossed the Circle C outfit. The lump in his throat choked him. He swallowed painfully, aware of the deep pity in Ruth Merrill's eyes as she moved toward the garden gate with his mother.

Alamo stood in grim silence, leaning on his long rifle, keen eyes studying him. Donal felt the impact of that analyzing look, sensed what was in Alamo's mind. He was probing for the steel that should be there—the high courage that had been his father's, the fortitude that could withstand the shock of disaster and grief.

His shoulders straightened and his chin lifted, and when he spoke his voice had the quietness of a man in complete control of himself.

"Where's Placido? Has he quit?"

"Quit nothin'." Brasca's look went to the barn door. "Comin' on the run. Reckon he was up the loft an' didn't see you ride in."

The choreman came slopping across the muddy yard. He was middle-aged and paunchy, and breathless from haste and excitement.

"*Por Dios*!" He beamed at the tall young man, pressed a hand to his breast. "Thees 'eart go bang w'en I see you jus' now. *Valgame Dios*! Thees beeg day for rancho, señor."

"*Gracias*." Donal's grin was affectionate. "Give the horses a rub-down, Placido."

"*Si*." The Mexican's eyes widened as he looked at the mud-spattered horses. "Thees 'orse Rocking D, no?"

"It's all right," Donal reassured him. "Rocking D's owner is here." He turned on his heel with a beckoning glance at the other two men.

Alamo's face wore a contented look as he moved with his loose-jointed stride up the worn flagstones to the *galeria*. He had just glimpsed the good hard metal of a man who could face death and disaster with unfaltering courage.

4

There was a somber look to the big living room now deep in shadows. Donal stood with his back to the great fireplace, his gaze playing over the faces of the others there. He was aware of a quickening pulse. He sensed in these silently waiting men a tension that needed only the right word from him to surge into unleashed action.

The thought both chilled and warmed him. He stood now where his father had stood. These men looked to him for leadership. For better or for worse, Circle C's fate was in his keeping.

His mother and Ruth Merrill came in. The girl was wearing a dress of some soft dark blue material, supplied from his mother's wardrobe, he guessed. How alike they were—the same slim grace of strong, supple body. It was amazing to him how well his mother had kept her youth.

His gaze followed them as they moved to a sofa under a window. The change from blue jeans and flannel shirt to feminine attire made a startling transformation in Ruth Merrill. She seemed taller, and indescribably lovely.

Marica Torres bustled in, uttered an ejaculation and went to the big crystal chandelier and lighted the lamp.

Donal saw Alamo look at the windows as the

mellow golden light drove back the encroaching darkness. The same thought was in his own mind. He glanced at one of the cowboys, sitting stiffly erect in a straight-backed chair.

"Pull the curtains, Dave," he said.

The cowboy obeyed, made the round of the windows. He was young, with a sunburned face and a shock of pale straw-colored hair. He seemed painfully conscious of the young girl sitting on the sofa with Mrs. Cameron, flushed a brick red as he passed in front of her and met her mildly curious look.

Mrs. Cameron broke the silence. She spoke quietly, a touch of hardness in her voice. "Rusty Cross was murdered last night," she began. "We have lost an old and loyal friend." She faltered, her troubled eyes going from face to face. "I wanted to talk to you about it. You see, I have reason to believe it is only the beginning of dreadful times for us—for Circle C . . . more killings, perhaps."

"Ma'am—" An elderly, heavy-shouldered man spoke earnestly in a raspy voice. "Circle C ain't never backed off from a fight no time."

Mrs. Cameron smiled faintly. "I'm not thinking of you, Bearcat. You and Brasca were fighting for Circle C before I came here to live."

"Our horns is mebbe some mossy, but we keep 'em plenty sharp," growled Brasca, nodding his grizzled head.

"I'm not worrying about you two old-timers," repeated Mrs. Cameron. Her gaze moved slowly from face to face. "Most of you boys have seen only easy times here at Circle C ranch. No rustlers, no fighting. Only the ordinary day by day work of the range." She hesitated, went on slowly, as if carefully choosing her words. "I have no cause to doubt any of you. It is only that I want you to know what we are in for. I won't hold it against any man here if he does not want to face it and prefers to say *adios* to Circle C and ride away."

There was a deep stillness, broken by a grunt from Bearcat. He got to his feet, stood on wide-apart bowlegs, thumbs hooked over gun belt, gaze roving belligerently around the room. "I reckon Circle C figgers to carry on," he said bluntly. "Any feller that figgers different 'ud better fork his bronc an' hightail it a long ways from the Rio Seco effen he ain't cravin' for his skelp to dangle from my belt."

A shrill chorus of yipping yells greeted his challenge. Bearcat grinned, resumed his chair. "I reckon you ain't got no call to worry about *this* outfit, ma'am," he chuckled.

"No—" Mrs. Cameron's voice was low, husky with emotion. "I believe you, Bearcat, and I—I'm proud of you all."

"We kin outride an' outfight any damn outfit in the hull Rio Seco," loudly declared Brasca.

"What all is this trouble that's on the prod our way, ma'am? From your talk I figger you got some idee 'bout what's back of ol' Rusty gittin' killed."

"Only this—" Mrs. Cameron touched a letter lying in her lap. "It came several weeks ago. I didn't worry about it then, but now—well—I don't know." She picked up the letter, held it out. "You read it aloud, Don."

Donal took the letter and moved closer to the lamp. He was already acquainted with its contents. His mother had shown it to him earlier in the afternoon. Alone in the ranch office she had listened quietly to his account of those last hours with his father on the rugged battle ground of San Juan Hill. She had wept a little, then resolutely given her attention to the more immediate problem of the mysterious attack upon himself and its possible connection with Ruth Merrill and her slain father. There was no doubt in her mind of what lay behind the murder of Circle C's foreman.

"This thing has been brewing for some time," she told her son. "In some way they learned that you were coming home, either you or your father. It was evident they were not sure, your names being the same. The trap was set for whichever one of you came up the trail. It was you, and they were going to kill you." She drew a long breath. "The name of Donal Cameron is a power in the Rio Seco and they wanted to wipe it out, leave themselves a free field. For the same reason they murdered Rusty Cross, your father's closest friend. Rusty would have been almost as dangerous to their plans. He had to be removed and news of the return of Donal Cameron was the signal."

It was then, in response to his bewildered questions, that she showed him the letter.

He stood there, his face a stern mask under the lamplight, brows bent frowningly at the letter in his hand. "It's signed by a man named Salvador Antista," he told his attentive listeners. "No envelope, nothing to give us an idea where it came from." Donal paused, sent an inquiring look at his mother. "You didn't say how it came."

"Marica found it in a box of supplies sent in from the Trading Post," she replied.

"Rod Dhu wouldn't have sent you a thing like this," puzzled Donal.

"It could have been slipped into the box without anybody noticing," Mrs. Cameron suggested.

"That's right." Donal shrugged, began to read the letter in a tight, angry voice.

> Mrs. Cameron:
>
> You won't be seeing Don and the kid again. They won't be back in the Rio Seco no more. We'll see to that, and this is a warning for you to pack up and get

> out. You Camerons have lived in the Rio Seco too long. You won't have a chance to buck us. You'll be sorry if you try. And if you don't know it, Don Cameron never was legal owner of the ranch. The Salazar woman he paid the money to wasn't Fidel Salazar's legal heir and the deed she signed was no good. Don Fidel's real heir was his brother, Mario Salazar who lived in Mexico City. Mario's daughter was my mother, and that makes me, Salvador Antista, the legal owner of the ranch you call yours. Be warned, pack and leave.

Donal folded the piece of paper and put it in his pocket. "If it were not for what happened to me today, and Rusty being murdered, I'd say the man is crazy," he said gloomily.

"Sounds loco for sure," agreed Alamo Jones. "Don't seem natcheral for a feller to put his name to a thing like that. Lays him wide open for the sheriff to throw him in jail." Alamo untangled his long legs, shambled over to the fireplace and spat delicately into the gray ashes. "Tell you what, son—" He gnawed reflectively at a short piece of plug tobacco. "It's my bet thar ain't no sich feller as this a-here Salvador Antista, and—"

Marica Torres interrupted him. "No, no, señor! You mooch wr-rong! Salvador Antista ees son of Mario Salazar's daughter. *Si*, I know." She hesitated, added uneasily, "Pasqual say 'e 'ave see thees Salvador Antista in San Benito."

Donal stared at her. "You mean Pasqual has talked with him?" He spoke in Spanish.

"I do not think Pasqual talked with him," replied Marica. "Pasqual seemed much troubled—and puzzled. He said it was an affair he did not understand and that he must talk with Antista."

"Where is Pasqual?" Donal frowned. "He should be here."

"He wasn't knowin' you was back, Don," Bearcat said. "We was over in the tule swamp, huntin' sign for the feller that killed Rusty. He headed for San Benito, said he'd pick up the mail."

Alamo broke the silence. "Waal, seems like I figgered some wrong about this a-here Antista feller." He chewed reflectively for a moment. "Only one thing to do . . . pick up his trail and git him throwed in jail."

"I reckon he's the feller that killed Rusty," growled Bearcat.

"We don't know," Donal argued. "I've an idea there's a lot going on we don't understand." He looked at Alamo. "What puzzles me is where Rocking D fits in. Miss Merrill claims her father has been murdered, and the murder made to appear an accident. This Antista business only adds to the mystery. Why was I waylaid and taken to Rocking D? Where does Colonel Merrill fit into the picture and why was he murdered?" Donal glanced at the girl on the sofa. "What was the danger that Ruth was running from, Alamo, and where do *you* fit in?" His slow smile softened the words. "It's mighty lucky for me you were standing watch at that gate. I'd not be here now if you hadn't mixed in."

"It weren't chance, me bein' thar at the gate when Ferrel fotched you in," drawled Alamo. "I l'arned they was layin' for you, or your dad. Didn't know which one of you would be along. I weren't goin' to set thar an' let Anse Jasey's gang do another murder. I was owin' your dad a debt. He saved my life back in the old days on the Brazos."

"How did it happen you were there at Rocking D?" asked Donal. "You seemed to be pretty thick with Ferrel." He stared curiously at the gaunt, bearded man. "You had me fooled, at first."

"I had 'em all fooled," chuckled Alamo. He flicked a glance at the silently attentive girl on the sofa. "All of 'em 'cept Ruth. She knowed what I was up to."

Ruth Merrill nodded her dark head. "Alamo came with us from New Orleans," she said.

"Sure," interrupted Alamo. He spoke gravely. "The colonel got uneasy 'bout the ranch . . . figgered Al Gober was some careless, or crooked, the way Rockin' D cows was gittin' lost off the range. He had me jine up with the outfit. Didn't let on to Al Gober that I was the colonel's friend. Made out I was on the dodge from the law for rustlin' cows down in the Nueces country." He gave his listeners a wintry smile. "Gober swallered the bait the way a calf goes for its mammy's milk."

Donal stood there, looking at him, his confused mind trying to make sense of the thing. Alamo's laconic explanation left him groping in the dark. He put his thoughts into words.

"I still don't see the connection between Rocking D and Circle C," he complained. "Why did Al Gober set that trap for me, and what's the truth behind Rusty's murder? I can understand now why Colonel Merrill was murdered. Gober probably suspected he was being investigated. It wouldn't be the first time a crooked foreman killed his suspicious boss. But I don't see where Circle C is involved."

"That's whar Anse Jasey comes in," Alamo told him grimly.

"Who is this Anse Jasey? He seems to be running things at Rocking D."

Isabel Cameron answered him. "Mr. Jasey is quite a newcomer to San Benito," she said. There was incredulity in her quiet voice. "It seems unbelievable that Mr. Jasey is mixed up in this dreadful affair. Why—he's been here several times—had luncheon with me."

"Jasey's a mighty slick gent," admitted Alamo. "You wouldn't think to look at him, hear him talk, that he's a pizen snake."

Mrs. Cameron stared at him, alarm growing in her eyes. "He was here a week ago, asking questions about the ranch," she said worriedly. "I—I thought he was just being friendly, interested in cattle conditions." She gave her son a panicky look. "I told him we were gathering a herd at Sheep Springs camp for shipment to Kansas City."

Alamo wagged his bearded face gravely. "That's sure too bad," he said. "You see, ma'am, Jasey is figgerin' to run things in the Rio Seco. Thar won't be no Circle C when he gits done his dirty work, nuther will thar be any Rockin' D outfit. Me an' the colonel was all set to git him throwed in jail for rustlin'. Jasey was too slick an' got the colonel afore we could play our ace card." Alamo paused, gave Ruth Merrill a compassionate look. "Ain't got proof that Jasey was back of the killin'. We found the colonel drowned in the crik . . . had a bruise on the side of his head like he had been thrown by his bronc and kicked. That's what Gober claimed . . . said it was an accident."

"It could have been an accident," Donal said thoughtfully. "It's going to be hard to prove it was murder."

Alamo shook his head. "Like I told you, I ain't

got proof that Jasey was back of it, but I sure know it weren't no accident. That bruise weren't from no horse kick. I've seen too many jaspers knocked cold with a gun barrel not to know *that* kind of bruise."

There was a silence. Alamo spoke again, slowly, almost pleadingly, as if determined they should realize the perilous situation that confronted him. "Weren't nothin' I could do. Had to figger some way to git Ruth away from thar and dassent show my hand to Gober. Would have been awful tough for Ruth to be left alone with that bunch of killers."

"You've been splendid," the girl said softly.

Alamo grinned at her. "Waal—I sure done some thinkin'," he said. "That's what your pa fotched me along for." His look shifted to Donal. "Was all set for us to git away the night afore you showed up at the gate. Heard Gober an' Ferrel talkin' over the plan to lay in the trail for Don Cameron. I told Ruth an' she said for us to set tight for a few hours an' see what the play was." Alamo chuckled. "I reckon you know the rest of it, son."

Donal was looking at Ruth Merrill. He was owing her a lot. Had it not been for her courageous decision there would have been no Alamo waiting at the yard gate.

She read his thought, smiled gravely. "Nothing could have dragged Alamo away at that moment," she said. "It would have been useless for me to tell him not to wait. I wasn't a bit brave about it. Those were the longest hours I ever spent—waiting for Alamo."

"Waal," drawled Alamo, "seems like I weren't needed at that. Don was all set to break away from there."

"Thanks to those trick knots," grinned Donal. He fell silent, fingers shaping a cigarette, his eyes narrowed in thought. He seemed to have suddenly withdrawn from them; and watching him, Isabel Cameron was conscious of a thrill. So often had she seen his father in that same withdrawn attitude while his coolly functioning brain attacked some problem. Brasca and Bearcat were watching him expectantly. They, too, were familiar with the signs. This young son of the beloved boss they would see no more was putting on his war paint.

"Brasca—" He spoke curtly. "I'm sending you to town. If you meet Pasqual heading for the ranch, tell him to go back to town with you and wait for me at the Trading Post." He paused, his eyes cold and hard on the grizzled cowboy. "Understand?"

Brasca nodded. "I savvy, boss—" His own eyes sent back an answering signal.

"If you don't meet him on the trail, look him up in town, any place he'd be likely to go."

"I savvy," repeated Brasca. He got to his feet,

shaggy brows drawn down in a questioning scowl. "What do I do if I don't find Pasqual no place?"

"Stick around in San Benito until I get there," Donal told him. "And Brasca, keep your ears and eyes wide open."

"My ears are plenty big," grinned the cowboy, "an' I ain't got to wearin' specs yet. You kin lay your cards on me, boss."

Donal gave him a brief answering smile in which there was no mirth. His gaze fastened on Bearcat. "You and the boys get ready for a ride," he said. "We're heading for the Sheep Springs camp. Tell Placido to throw my saddle on old Stormy." His look swept the intent faces of the other men. "All right, boys, hop to it."

Chairs scraped back, booted feet went pounding into the hall. Donal's appraising look followed the men trooping at Bearcat's heels. He was conscious of a pride in them. His father, and Rusty, had hand-picked these hard-bitten riders. There had never been a place for weaklings on Circle C's payroll—nor for treachery. The last thought sent a stab that hurt. Not Pasqual Torres! He must keep that suspicion crushed. Marica's son could not be a traitor. Pasqual was a Circle C man, and no Circle C man had ever stooped to treachery.

His mother and Ruth Merrill were on their feet, their eyes intent on him. Marica Torres, standing near the hall door, lifted her arms tragically. "*Señor*"—she spoke frantically in Spanish—"you think bad things about my Pasqual!"

Mrs. Cameron saw his distress. "Don't be silly, Marica. Nobody has said a word about Pasqual." She slipped a hand under the housekeeper's arm and led her from the room.

Donal watched them go, his face troubled. Ruth Merrill broke the silence.

"Why did she say that?" she asked in a mystified voice.

Donal shook his head. He stood there, wordless, his eyes cold in the hard mask of his face. It was Alamo who answered her.

"I figger she knows somethin' she ain't wantin' to tell," he said drily. "Don't it hit you that way, son?"

"I'm not saying," Donal replied gloomily. "Pasqual has been with us since he was a kid. I'm not going to accuse him unheard. I'm worried about him, yes—but for reasons I don't want his mother to suspect."

Alamo nodded gravely. "I reckon I savvy, son. You figger that mebbe he's layin' dead some place, huh?"

"It's easier to think that—than to think the other thing of him," replied Donal.

Alamo's jaws worked meditatively. "Ain't knowin' this Pasqual feller," he said. "I figger he was on to somethin' an' it's a even bet he's talked about it to his ma from the way she went an' jumped you." He paused, added apologetically, "I'm thinkin' out loud, son—"

"Keep on talking," Donal said, grimly.

"Waal, I see it this way," Alamo went on; "the thing points back to Anse Jasey. He's usin' this Salvador Antista jasper for a blind . . . had it all figgered to wipe you out same as he fixed your foreman. Would have made it easy for him if he could scare your ma so bad she would clear out of the Rio Seco." Alamo nodded his head. "Take it from me, son—Jasey is usin' this Antista jasper for a stalkin' horse."

"You think that Antista killed Rusty?"

Alamo shook his head. "Ain't likely, son. It's my bet Antista don't know Jasey's usin' him for poison bait. He's been filled up with a lot of talk that he's old Don Fidel's true heir an' that if he plays the cards the way Jasey deals 'em he'll git to be owner of Circle C." His shrewd eyes narrowed thoughtfully. "Brasca won't be meetin' Pasqual on the home trail, son. I'm gamblin' that Pasqual is already layin' dead some place, or that Jasey has him hid away—along with Antista."

"I'd rather think that, than think the other thing of him," Donal said again. The pain in him looked from his eyes. "Though God knows the last is bad enough," he added miserably. "We've got to work fast, Alamo." His look went to Ruth Merrill, lingered. "I'm sorry—" The words stumbled awkwardly from him. "I'm not meaning to forget your own troubles."

Her hand lifted in a protesting gesture. "My troubles are tied up with yours," she said. "It's my fight, too—"

His eyes thanked her, and after a moment he said to Alamo, "Don't know when I'll be back—"

Alamo nodded. "Sure. I savvy, son, an' don't you fret none. I'll stick here close . . . keep a eye on things."

"*Gracias.*" Donal gave him a warm look. "You're a good friend, Alamo."

"The best in the world," Ruth Merrill said softly. "I should know."

He grinned at them, wagged his grizzled beard. "You doggone kids, ain't nothin' I like so good as a fight. I was born the night my pappy got killed 'longside Davy Crockett, which is why I got to be called Alamo." He chuckled grimly. "You git started for that cow camp at Sheep Springs, son. I'll stick close on the job here."

Donal was doing some quick thinking. "I'll leave Bearcat and a couple of boys with you," he decided. His eyes met the girl's look. "You're right," he told her. "We are in this thing together. I won't be forgetting you while I'm gone."

She gave him a grave little smile. "I remember an old letter from Grand-uncle Daker. He was once an enemy of your father's . . . tried to run him out of the Rio Seco country. Your father wouldn't run and he and grand-uncle became firm friends. We have inherited that friendship. I'm trusting you to the limit, Donal Cameron."

"There is no limit," Donal said simply. The hard look had gone from his eyes, and his slow, warming smile put color into her cheeks.

"No limit," she echoed softly, "*Adios*, Donal—" She was suddenly at his side, her hand in his. "Good luck ride with you!"

Spurs jingled in the hall, and they saw Bearcat in the doorway, bowlegs wide apart, thumbs hooked over gun belt, a wide grin on his leathery face.

"All set, boss," he reported.

Donal hesitated. It was going to be hard to disappoint the veteran Circle C man. He said slowly, "We can't leave the place unprotected, Bearcat—"

"Huh!" Bearcat looked at him suspiciously.

"That's right," grinned Donal. "You are elected to stay with Alamo. . . . You and a couple of the boys."

"Doggone," grumbled the cowboy. "You would go an' pick on me." His look went to the girl, met her faint smile. The impact seemed to dull the edge of his disappointment. His face brightened. "Sure, boss. Reckon it's a right smart idee," he rumbled. "No tellin' but what that killer is still layin' 'round some place, waitin' to git hisself another skelp."

Ruth repressed a shiver, and Alamo Jones said drily, “He won’t be takin’ no more skelps, not with me an’ you keepin’ lookout.”

Donal moved to the door, paused and looked back at the girl. “Don’t let Bearcat’s talk frighten you.” He smiled reassuringly. “There’s no danger—if you keep close to the house.” He disappeared into the hall.

Mrs. Cameron was in the kitchen, comforting a tearful Marica. The sharp clatter of his bootheels drew her outside in time to see his tall shape push through the gate. She ran quickly down the path, stood watching the group of riders gathered there under the starlight. She saw Donal swing into his saddle and the riders move on across the yard. Perhaps Donal sensed her presence. He swung his horse and rode toward her. She ran to meet him and he bent low, kissed her. No words passed between them, and in a moment he was spurring to overtake the others.

For long minutes Mrs. Cameron stood there, listening to the fading hoofbeats. A voice spoke softly from the darkness behind her.

“Don’t you git to fearin’ for him, ma’am.”

She turned slowly and looked at the tall shape standing by the garden gate.

“He’s riding Stormy,” she said, her voice not quite steady. “His—his father’s horse.”

“Sure.” Alamo nodded approvingly. “Like Bearcat said back thar in the house, Don figgers to carry on the way his dad would. He's boss now, ma'am, and I reckon Circle C is plenty safe in his hands."

"Pray God you are right, Alamo," Mrs. Cameron said in a voice that was hardly more than a whisper. She smiled at him, a hint of tears in her eyes.

5

The smoke curling from the cabin chimney seemed to fascinate the lone watcher on the bluffs some three hundred yards away. There was yearning in his hard eyes. He knew the reputation of the man down there in that cabin. Flapjack Skeeters was the best camp cook in the Rio Seco. Flapjack could turn out a pan of hot biscuit as light as angels' wings, and his gravy was a hungry cowboy's dream of what gravy should be.

The man on the bluffs swore feelingly. Looking at that thin blue haze of smoke filled him with griping hunger pains. He could fairly smell the tantalizing odors of juicy steaks sizzling in Flapjack's big pan.

The spy stifled a groan, sat back on his heels and gloomily fumbled cigarette papers and tobacco from his shirt pocket. Nothing to do but wait for word from Al Gober. It had been one hell of a day, what with the drenching rain of the early morning and losing his lunch some place back on the trail. The packet of sandwiches must have slipped out of his rolled-up slicker when he got down to untie it from his saddle.

He lit the cigarette, sullen, watchful eyes on the scene below. A herd of cattle was moving slowly up the narrow valley that funneled between low-lying hills.

The rain had settled the dust and cleared the air. He could see the white faces of the bawling cattle and knew them for what they were. Prime three-year-old steers that wore the Circle C brand on their hides. They were the reason for his long day's vigil on the bluff overlooking Sheep Springs camp.

A lone rider preceded the herd, his horse moving at a fast shuffling walk to the corral where a blind-folded gray mare was hitched to a big pump. Water gushed into the trough as the mare plodded patiently around the deeply-rutted circular path. The trough, a long one, extended under the wire fence to a muddy pond. Once, the mare halted, and warned by the sudden quiet of the creaky pump the cook appeared in the doorway of the cabin and yelled at her shrilly. The mare resumed her slow walk and again the water poured out in jerky gushes.

Three other riders trailed the herd, yipping at the stragglers; and suddenly aware of the water the steers broke into a lumbering run. In a few minutes they stood belly-deep in the pond, crowding in close, flank to flank.

The cook again appeared in the doorway, a cigarette under an untidy grizzled mustache, a long fork in one hand. He stood watching while the four riders rode into the corral.

Salty nodded, gestured in the direction of the brush-covered slope under the high bluff that concealed the interested spy. “Couple of you fellers go snake in some of that piñon,” he ordered.

Two of the cowboys swung back to their saddles and started away. Flapjack’s shrill voice followed them.

“Make it snappy,” he called. “I’m ’bout ready to throw the steaks in the pan.”

One of the pair, a slim, black-haired youth, grinned back at him. “Figger to have biscuit for supper, Flapjack?”

“Sure do, Chico,” answered the cook. He disappeared inside the cabin.

Chico let out a shrill yip and jumped his horse into a dead run toward the piñon scrub. “Come on, Shorty,” he yelled to his companion. “You heard what Flapjack said!”

The lone watcher on the bluff cursed under his breath. For two cents he’d sneak down there and help himself to Flapjack’s hot biscuit and gravy and steaks. He’d put his gun on that damn Circle C bunch . . . make ’em stand there like fools while he filled his aching belly.

Salty’s voice reached him through the clear air, jerked his thoughts away from food.

“Sure is mighty queer, Rusty not showin’ up,” worried the Circle C cattle boss. He was a leathery-faced man of middle height and years. He was competent looking and wore a sandy mustache that drooped over a good-humored mouth. "Cain't figger out why Rusty didn't get here like he promised." Salty pulled the saddle from his sweat-grimed horse. "What you make of it, Omaha?"

Omaha dropped the bridle from his horse, stood rubbing a calloused thumb over a cracked buckle while he considered the question.

The cattle boss grunted and walked off to the corral fence with his saddle. He knew Omaha's peculiarities too well to press him for an answer. Omaha liked to think a thing out before expressing an opinion. He was a cautious man with words, though he could be fast enough when it came to physical action.

Salty threw the damp saddle across the fence rail and stood fumbling with cigarette papers and tobacco. Omaha waddled up, saddle slung over a shoulder. He was a wiry little man in his middle fifties, and a lifetime in the saddle had given him a pair of bowlegs that were the pride of the outfit.

He slung his gear over the fence rail, frowned thoughtfully at the bridle draped over the saddle horn. "Buckle's sure busted to hell," he grunted. "Got to fix me a new one after supper." He reached into a pocket and drew out a piece of plug tobacco, gnawed off a generous chew and carefully pushed the tobacco back into his pocket. "Ain't likin' it," he said. "You was askin' me, Salty, an' that thar's my answer." He rubbed the enormous grizzled mustache that bisected his lean dark face. "I smell trouble, plenty trouble."

Salty stared at him in grim silence. He had a vast respect for Omaha's opinions. He knew from experience that Omaha was usually right.

His look shifted to the steers milling in the pond. A rich prize, those more than six hundred prime steers. The possibilities put a glacier look in his eyes. He said slowly, "How come you get that notion, Omaha?"

Omaha chewed on his cud reflectively, spat a dark brown stream. "Me and you has knowed Rusty Cross a lot of years," he said. "Rusty figgered to be here at the camp by noon. He ain't showed up, and he ain't sent no word why he ain't showed up. It ain't like Rusty. He'd be here, or he'd have sent word."

"Meanin' he's run into trouble, huh?" Fast-growing alarm put a rasp in Salty's voice.

"It adds up thataways, same as two and two tote four," rejoined Omaha.

The cattle boss gestured fiercely. "My Gawd, only four of us here to put up a fight."

"Five, countin' Flapjack," reminded Omaha. "Flapjack can do a awful lot of damage with that sawed-off shotgun he lays sich store by."

Salty Wells nodded gloomily, his gaze on the two younger men approaching with bundles of dry piñon dragging at the ends of their ropes. The cook appeared in the doorway. "Come an' git it, or she goes out the winder," he bellowed.

Chico and Shorty slid from their horses, fingers jerked at saddle leathers. The cattle boss spoke brusquely. "Hold it, boys!"

They stared back at him with shocked eyes. Salty was already moving toward the horse corral. "Throw your saddles on fresh broncs," he called over his shoulder. He snatched up his rope and headed for a tall roan that began sidling away, distrustful of the slow-swinging loop.

Omaha reached for his own rope and waddled into the corral, and, after an exchange of dismayed looks, the two cowboys ran to the bundles of piñon and jerked their ropes loose.

Flapjack's scowling face appeared in the doorway. He was a range-seasoned old-timer and one quick look at Salty Wells was enough. Concern replaced the annoyance on his weathered visage. Something was wrong. He smelled trouble as surely as he smelled the fragrance of the rich brown gravy in his kettle. With a grunt he turned from the doorway and limped to the sawed-off shotgun that leaned in a corner of the room. It wouldn't be the first time he had met trouble head-on. It was a rustler's bullet that had ended his riding days and made him the best camp cook in the Rio Seco.

The man on the bluff watched the flurry of excitement with undisguised interest, a sour grin on his face. He had overheard enough to make a shrewd guess that the non-appearance of Rusty

Cross was the cause of that excitement. The spy chuckled in his throat. He could give that damn Salty Wells a piece of news about Rusty Cross that would stand his hair on end.

He continued to watch, cigarette smoke curling from hairy nostrils. The ground, where he lay on his spread-out slicker, was littered with countless cigarette stubs. The man glanced at them sourly, snubbed out the one in his fingers and added it to the heap. His last smoke. Not enough tobacco left in his sack to put in his eye. He muttered an oath and got stiffly to his feet. Lying there so long had put a cramp in his legs. No sense staying, soon be too dark to use his eyes, and anyway it was about time he headed for the rendezvous.

He took a look at the camp, now shadowed in the deepening twilight. The four Circle C men were riding their fresh horses toward the cabin where Flapjack stood in the doorway. He could hear the cook's husky voice bawling at them. "Ain't keepin' supper for you jaspers all night," warned Flapjack with an indignation that was only pretense. He knew well enough that only an extreme crisis could have caused the delay. But a camp cook worth his salt had to bear down hard on discipline. The boys would have thought him a sick man if he failed to show a proper spirit.

"Sure am sorry, Flapjack," apologized Salty. "At that, we ain't got much time to eat."

The cook gave him a shrewd look, nodded and

vanished inside. They heard the slam of tin plates snatched hot from the oven.

"You boys fill up quick," the cattle boss told his companions. "I'm stickin' with the herd till you get finished."

"You bet," chorused Chico and Johnny. They clattered into the room. Salty's voice held Omaha for a moment. "Tell Flapjack to fix me up a sandwich," the cattle boss said. "Soon as you boys get done eatin' we're spreadin' them steers back on the range." He swore softly. "Mebbe I'm a fool, but if you're right about Rusty it sure looks like hell is due to bust loose at this cow camp."

"You'd be a damn fool if you don't spread 'em," Omaha said with a bleak smile. "Right now that bunch of steers is a rustler's dream." Spurs dragging, he hurried to join Chico and Shorty at the table.

Salty swung his horse, reined in short as Flapjack suddenly reappeared.

"Figgered you'd have time to swaller a cup of hot coffee," the cook said. "Fetched you a steak sandwich."

"*Gracias*," grinned the cattle boss. He drained the cup, handed it back and took the huge sandwich in both hands. The cook watched him with shrewd eyes. Salty swallowed a mouthful of sandwich, met his inquiring gaze. His own eyes narrowed as a sudden thought struck him.

"Flapjack," he said softly, "soon as the boys get done eatin', you take your blanket roll and go hole up some place. Ain't carin' for the signs right now."

The cook jerked an understanding nod. His expression grim, he swung on his heel and limped back to his stove. Salty rode over to the pump and halted the gray mare. He slid from his saddle, slipped her collar and bridle and sent her off with a gentle slap on the rump.

The man on the bluff was crawling cautiously through the brush. His head lifted for a look down at the camp, now withdrawing behind the darkening veil of night. Only the glimmer of lamplight from the cabin, and Chico's voice lifted in loud and admiring comment: "Doggone, Flapjack! You sure can ride a biscuit pan—"

The spy's lips twisted in a malevolent grin. "Eat hearty, feller," he muttered. "You won't git no more chance to fill yore belly." Suddenly reckless, he stood upright, went pushing quickly through the scrub toward his concealed horse. A piñon branch snapped underfoot with the report of a pistol shot.

The sound faintly touched Salty's ears. He stiffened in his saddle, stared with wary, uneasy eyes at the bluffs, now formless and forbidding in the blanketing night.

6

The black horse under him stirred Donal's imagination. His father had trained Stormy from colt days and broken him to the saddle. The black had always been a one-man horse, resentful of any stranger on his back. His quiet acceptance of Donal was startling, tingled the young cowman's blood, gave him the queer feeling that his father shared the saddle with him and that the sensitive black horse knew it.

The half score riders trailing Donal exchanged wondering comment. Most of them knew from personal experience that Stormy was too much for the best rider in the outfit. They regarded him as an outlaw so far as they were concerned.

"Cain't figger it out," puzzled one of the cowboys. "I forked that piece of black dynamite one time and he pitched me so high I sure played peek-a-boo with the stars." He reined his horse around a fallen log. "How do you figger it, Dave?"

"I reckon he's got old Stormy fooled," speculated Dave. "Don is the spittin' image of the old man. Same build, same voice, and sits a saddle the same way." The blond cowboy grinned. "I reckon that's the answer, Scarface. That black horse don't savvy no difference between Don and his dad."

Scarface grunted skeptically. He was a chunky, efficient-looking man with a swarthy face permanently marked by a knife-throwing half-breed rustler. He cocked an appraising eye at the pale glow stealing over the mountains. "Moonlight, time we hit the ridge," he said.

The trail left the canyon floor and climbed the steep slope in a series of hairpin turns that left the horses blowing hard by the time they reached the summit.

The valley lay below them, a place of vague lights and shadows under the moon. No sound broke the nocturnal hush, only the labored breathing of the winded horses, the faint far-away wail of a locomotive.

Don winced. His father had worked hard to persuade the railroad to run that spur across the lower valley. He had not lived to see its completion, nor the little town of Cameron that had sprung up at the end of rail. The project would practically eliminate the long, arduous drives and was a boon to every cowman in the Rio Seco country. Also it was the reason why the once remote camp at Sheep Springs had assumed a new importance as the gathering place for all Circle C steers ready for shipment. An easy day's drive could put them in the loading pens at Cameron, in prime condition for the Eastern markets. The long trail drives were a thing of the past.

Donal gazed down into the valley, aware of a vague uneasiness. Something seemed wrong with the picture. Too quiet down there in the valley. It was Dave Herne who put his finger on the cause of his growing alarm.

"Should be cows bawlin'," the blond cowboy remarked. "Looks like Salty didn't get them steers gathered."

"Sure is queer," muttered Scarface. "Cain't see the camp till we get round the bluff, but I'm bettin' we won't find no cows there."

Donal's look went to him, swept the faces of the other men. There was grim expectancy in their eyes, but no hint of fear. He said briefly, "Let's go, boys." They lined out along the trail that led to the high bluff. Spurs jingled, shod hoofs rattled on loose stones, a man cursed softly as his horse snorted and reared. "Only a doggone tarantula!" he scolded. "Quit your foolin', bronc."

From somewhere below the bluffs a gunshot shattered the deep quiet of the valley. The Circle C men halted their horses and Scarface said harshly, "Flapjack!"

"That sure was his old sawed-off shotgun," agreed Dave. "Looks like hell's bust loose down there, Don."

"Listen!" Donal gestured for silence. Men's voices reached to them through the night, indistinctly at first, and then a loud shout, "Let's set the damn shack afire!" Almost instantly the suggestion was challenged by another reverberating roar from Flapjack's shotgun.

Donal was off his horse, and sensing his purpose the Circle C men hurriedly slid from saddles. "One of you boys stay with the horses." Donal's look fastened on a slim young Mexican under an enormous steeple hat. "You, Epifanio. Bring 'em on the jump when I give you a yell."

"*Si, señor.*" Epifanio looked his disappointment. He wanted to go with them and try out the brand-new Winchester that Pasqual Torres had given him on his birthday, the last Blessed Epiphany. *Por Dios*, he was a grown man, and none better than himself with rope or gun.

Scarface, dragging his own rifle from saddle boot, threw him a sympathetic grin. "You'll smell plenty gunsmoke before this ball's done, kid," he prophesied grimly. "Take it easy, feller."

In a few moments, Epifanio was alone with the horses, listening to the yells and curses of the rustlers, punctuated by echoing crashes from the beleaguered cook's shotgun.

The Circle C men reached the fringing piñon scrub at the foot of the bluff. They could see the rustlers, vague, scurrying shapes in the moonlight, dragging piñon branches from Flapjack's woodpile and stacking them against the door. There were no windows in the front wall and they were safe enough from the raging cook's gunfire.

"Six of 'em," muttered Dave Herne, crouching

by Donal's side. His rifle lifted. Donal's gesture held his trigger-finger.

"I want 'em alive," he said. "They can tell me things I've got to know."

Matches spurted into flame from the group in front of the cabin. A voice shouted furiously, "Brush is too damn wet!" Another voice yelled, "Here's a can of coal oil settin' by the woodpile!" He snatched up the five gallon can and ran with it toward the heaped-up brush.

Donal's rifle lifted, spat flame, and with the crashing report the big can jerked from the man's hand. He came to an abrupt standstill, stared dazedly at the fallen can that was spurting kerosene from jagged bullet-torn holes.

Startled shouts broke the momentary hush. The dismayed rustlers came out of their paralysis and fled toward their horses bunched beyond the long water trough. Rifle-fire crackled from the piñon scrub below the bluff and one of the running men pitched headlong and slid to a sprawling heap on the ground. Another rustler took a flying leap over the water trough, groaned in midair and fell across the trough, kicking and shuddering. Three of his companions reached the snorting horses and tore off into the night, heads bent low over saddles, guns spurting flame back at their attackers.

The Circle C men broke into a run from the chaparral, and realizing that escape was hopeless the last member of the raiding party halted his dash across the yard and lifted his hands in surrender.

The cabin door banged open and Flapjack emerged, shouting sulphurous comments as he kicked his way through the piled-up brush.

Donal raced up to him. "Where's Salty?" he demanded, and then, not waiting for the cook's reply, he lifted his voice in a loud yell to Epifanio. "All right, kid . . . come on down with the horses!"

"*Si*, *señor*!" came the Mexican's shout.

Flapjack, breathing hard, stared past him at the captured rustler. "Was aimin' to fry me, the low-down skunks," he exploded. And then suddenly he was staring at Donal with incredulous eyes. "Doggone, when did *you* git back?"

"This morning," answered Donal. He repeated his question, "Where's Salty?"

The cook gestured vaguely. "Somewheres out thar, I reckon. Ain't seen him sence sundown." He continued to stare. "Doggone, son! It's sure good to see you." His delighted grin vanished and he added grimly, "Ain't knowin' for why, but hell's sure bust loose at this cow camp." The cook squinted a look at the dead man lying across the trough.

"Salty got some narvous, Rusty not showin' up at the camp, figgered only thing to do was to push the cows back on the range. He knowed that Rusty would have come, or sent word and figgered somethin' was awful wrong." Flapjack fingered a plug of tobacco from a pocket and gnawed off a chew reflectively. "Looks like Salty figgered right. Them damn rustlers sure would have had easy pickin's—them steers all gathered like they was."

"Only six of them," Donal said. "Salty and the boys could have stood them off."

"Six," snorted the cook. "I reckon there was close on a score of them doggone wolves. Most of 'em set off in chase of the cows." His leathery face crinkled in a contented grin. "Son, you should have heard the cussin' when that ornery bunch of rustlers rode in and found Salty had figgered the play and scattered them cows to hell and gone." Flapjack paused, scrutinized the group of Circle C men approaching with the prisoner. "How come Rusty ain't along?" he inquired.

"Rusty's dead," Donal told him. "Murdered—"

Flapjack gave him a shocked look. "Huh!" He wagged his head sadly. "That's sure bad news, Don." He glared balefully at the prisoner. "Reckon I savvy what brung you here on the jump."

"You don't know where Salty and the boys might be now?" questioned Donal.

Flapjack shook his head. "That bunch of cow thieves left here in a hurry when they found the herd gone," he answered. "No tellin' what's happened if they run into the boys."

Donal stared grimly at the rustler. "Any of you boys know this man?"

There was a shaking of heads. Donal moved closer to the man, looked him over carefully. "Who's your boss?"

The rustler kept his sullen silence, and Flapjack said harshly, "Git a rope around his neck. He'll mebbe find his tongue."

"No." Donal spoke curtly. "No necktie party. We've got laws for his kind."

"No tellin' but what that bunch of killers will be headin' back this way," reminded the cook. "You're outnumbered two to one." He grinned ruefully. "Salty told me to go hole up some place. Reckon I stuck around too long."

Donal came to a decision. "I'm sending you back to the ranch with him, Flapjack." His look went to the Mexican youth. "You'd better go with them, Epifanio."

"*Si, señor.*" Epifanio smiled thinly. "He will not escape, señor."

Flapjack looked dubious, but made no further protest. "Git a saddle throwed on my pinto, kid," he said to the Mexican. "I'll watch this jasper."

Dave said, "This feller's bronc stampeded with the rest of the bunch."

"There are horses in the corral," Donal said. "Get a saddle on one of them, Dave."

The cowboy hurried after Epifanio, and Donal took the cook aside. "Listen, Flapjack. I want this man delivered at the ranch *alive.*" There was a stern warning in his voice. "He can tell me, things—when he's ready to talk. Understand?"

The cook nodded gloomily. "I savvy." His smile was mirthless. "Figgerin' I'd mebbe deliver him dead, huh?" He scowled. "You ain't so fur wrong at that, Don. I ain't forgettin' they was all set to fry me in my own cook-shack."

"Listen," Donal said again. "You want to find out who killed Rusty Cross, don't you?"

"Sure do," grunted the cook. His eyes were cold glints in the moonlight.

"That is why we want this man kept alive. He knows who killed Rusty."

Flapjack's eyes gleamed. "Boss," he said earnestly, "you ain't got no more call to worry. That jasper ain't gittin' away from me, and he ain't gittin' hurt."

Donal turned to his horse and swung into the saddle.

"All right, boys."

They rode away from the cabin, halting briefly to drag the dead rustler from the water trough and lay him alongside his slain companion. Dave spurred from the corral on the horse he had saddled for the prisoner, changed to his own horse and hurried to overtake them. He drew alongside Donal. "Which way, boss?" He spoke worriedly. "Looks like Salty and the boys is cornered some place."

"Only thing we can do is look for them," Donal replied curtly. Dave gave him a brief glance, reined his horse a trifle and fell in with Scarface.

"The look on him give me the shivers," the blond cowboy muttered to his friend. "He's killin' mad."

"His dad was the same way," Scarface said. "He'd get a look on him like cold death." The swarthy cowboy gave his companion a wintry smile. "I'm only hopin' there's a feller that wears the name of Squint in that bunch we're trailin'," he added. "He's the half-breed skunk that slashed up my face."

It was useless to keep their horses moving faster than a walk. Their first object was to pick up a likely trail that would lead them to the missing Circle C men, or bring them in contact with the rustlers. They made frequent halts, ears keyed for any tell-tale sound in that moonlit stillness—a gunshot, the thud of hoofs.

The long valley widened before them, rough and boulder-strewn and laced with deep gullies, an inhospitable land, useless for any purpose except the ranging of cattle. To the west lifted the embattled crags of the Comanches, while to the east the terrain rapidly deteriorated into a vast and bewildering maze of deep gorges, deadly traps where a man could wander for days until overcome by hunger and thirst.

Donal knew that Salty Wells was a capable and shrewd-witted cowman. Once he had decided to scatter the steers he would make a good job of it. No man in the Rio Seco could compare with him in first-hand knowledge of the remote labyrinth known as the Devil's Hideout. Salty could find his way through those gorges in the dark.

Donal halted his horse, stared with frowning intentness at the dark outline of low hills to the east. He was conscious of a growing excitement. Salty would have put his knowledge of the Devil's Hideout to use, hide the cattle where the rustlers would fail to find them in a month of Sundays.

"Any of you boys know the Devil's Hideout country?" he asked.

Scarface's voice answered him. "Was over there a couple of times with Salty," he said. "Sure is hell's back yard . . . No place for a feller to get careless."

Donal made no comment. His gaze shifted down the moonlit valley. The faint wail of a locomotive touched their ears.

Dave Herne said speculatively, "I reckon that's a cattle train pullin' out of Cameron."

"Or an empty, pullin' in," suggested Scarface. "Cain't tell from here which way that train is headed."

Donal turned his head to look at him. "Think you can find your way into the Devil's Hideout?" His voice was thoughtful.

"Sure can," Scarface declared. Sudden excitement edged his voice. "I'm bettin' that's where Salty has high-tailed them cows to. Is that your notion, boss?"

"That's right," Donal admitted.

"There's a thousand holes he could hide them steers in," chuckled Scarface. "Salty showed me one place where there's plenty feed, and a spring. Queer place, shaped like a saucer with high cliffs a goat couldn't climb up or down. Only one narrow gap you can go in at. Couple of fellers could hold that place till hell froze if they didn't get starved out."

Donal nodded. He had heard Rusty and his father speak of the curious little rim-rocked oasis, a startling sight in the bleak heart of that wilderness of desolation.

"You're elected to have a look over there, Scarface," he said. "All of you, except Dave. I'm taking Dave with me."

They stared at him, surprised, bewildered. They considered the problem of where to find the vanished herd solved. Why look further when the answer lay in the direction of the Devil's Hideout?

He read the question in their eyes, shook his head. "No, I'm not crazy. There's a chance the rustlers headed toward Cameron. They might gamble that Salty went that way. It's worth taking a look."

"You'll sure run into plenty trouble, if your guess is right," argued Scarface. "That's a bad bunch."

"We'll be seeing them first," smiled Donal. He looked at Dave. "You don't *have* to come with me, Dave."

"H-hell!" stuttered the blond cowboy. "Y-you ain't s-stoppin' me."

"*Bueno.*" Donal grinned. "All set, boys. Keep your eyes peeled. If Salty has the herd over there you'll pick up sign easy enough." He hesitated. "If you find Salty, tell him I said to hold the herd there until I show up, and tell him to post a lookout for me." He chuckled. "I've never seen that little stone corral you described, Scarface. Sounds like a fairy tale."

"I seen it with my own eyes," insisted the cowboy. "Grass knee high, and cold water bubblin' out of a cliff. Sure made my eyes pop when I rode into that devil's parlor with Salty."

"I'm believing you," laughed Donal. His hand lifted in a parting gesture. "Come on, Dave."

Stirrup to stirrup, the pair pushed on through the moonlight toward Cameron.

7

Early dawn brought a low ground fog and the two men rode through a cold, blanketing grayness that seemed to hold the harsh landscape in a sinister hush. The poor visibility held them down to a slow walk.

Dave Herne began to fret. "Cain't see a thing in this fog," he complained. "We could be ridin' in circles and not know it."

"We're not far from the railroad," Donal said. "Listen—" His hand lifted, and from the right a muted rumble touched their ears.

Dave grinned his relief. "I reckon we ain't lost *yet,*" he said.

It was the sudden excitement of the black horse that warned them of the unseen riders. Donal correctly interpreted the meaning of the upflung head, the nervous twitch of ears.

They drew to a standstill, waited for some confirming sound. The horses fidgeted, turned their heads simultaneously, as if drawn on the same string, and stared off to the left, ears sharply forward.

"Horses," muttered Dave. "Headin' this way, sounds like." His hand slid down to gun-butt.

The thud of hoofs drifted nearer, and they heard the creak of saddle leather, the jingle of spurs. A rasping voice bitterly cursed the fog.

"I'm prayin' different," Dave muttered. "I ain't wantin' this fog to lift right now, not with that bunch so close."

They swung away to the right, pushed slowly through the blanketing mist and drew in behind a dense growth of creosote bushes. A puff of wind touched their faces. Donal gave his companion a grim smile. "*Adios*, fog," he said.

Rifts appeared in the gray pall and they caught a brief glimpse of slow-moving riders. Dave Herne swore under his breath. "Lucky for us we found cover," he said. "Close on twenty of 'em."

More rifts appeared, and suddenly the fog was gone, and sunlight flared over mountain ridges, lay bright, revealing fingers on the compact group of riders less than two hundred yards away.

Loud, wrangling voices reached through the thin air to the Circle C men behind the covering greasewood. It was apparent there was a disagreement among the rustlers. Donal cautiously stole a look.

There was no mistaking the man on the buckskin horse. He would not easily forget the death's head mask that Al Gober wore for a face.

Gober's long, gaunt frame sagged wearily in the saddle, hands resting on the horn while he listened in scowling silence to the bickering. It was plain that his balked plans, the long and fruitless night, were fuel for a wicked rage in him. He suddenly interrupted the argument.

"Quit your yelpin'," he said.

The cold ferocity in his voice brought an instant silence. Gober studied their intent faces, a scrutinizing, probing look that made some of them stir uneasily in their saddles. He gave them his sinister, mirthless smile. "I'm bossin' this show," he said.

Another long silence, broken by a resentful voice. "You're done with bossin' me, Gober. I'm fed up with sashayin' all over hell's back yard for them Circle C cows. Ain't no sense in us stickin' round here like a flock of damn fools. I'm for high-tailin' it from this range pronto while the goin's good."

Gober's eyes fastened on the speaker, a lean, wiry man with a hawk-like face that gave him a peculiarly bold and predatory look.

"Yeah?" Gober spoke gently. "Meanin' just what, Monte?"

"Meanin' I'm quittin' your damn job," announced the rebel. "I ain't stickin' round to run into a lot of Circle C lead."

"Sure—" Gober gave his death's head grin. "All right with me if you figger to quit, Monte." He gestured. "Go right ahead, feller. You can figger up what's comin' to you with Anse Jasey when you get back to town."

The man gave him a hard, bright look. "You bet I'm seein' Anse Jasey." He spoke bitterly. "Mebbe you think I ain't got the nerve, but I'm sure tellin' him plenty for the deal he handed me."

"Yeah?" Gober shook his head slowly, his smile widening. "I'd do just that, Monte. It was Anse hired you."

"He wasn't tellin' me it was cow stealin'," grumbled Monte. He glowered. "Well, so long, fellers. No hard feelin's." Hand lifting in a parting gesture he swung his horse away.

He was less than ten yards distant when Gober's hand swooped down, came up with a gun; and with the crashing report of the .45 the man pitched headlong from his saddle.

Smoking gun in lowered hand, Gober continued to stare off at his victim. There was no movement there, nothing to indicate that life remained in that sprawling heap lying in the shadow of a creosote bush.

A long moment passed. Gober slowly holstered the gun and looked at his companions. Their expressionless faces showed a callous indifference to the cowardly murder. One of them nodded approval, lips twisted in a wicked grin.

"You couldn't do nothin' else, Al. The yeller skunk got what was comin'."

Donal, watching the scene, recognized the speaker. The half-breed, Squint. His fingers tightened yearningly over gun-butt. It was an impulse he quickly crushed. The target was too far away, even for his long-barreled Colt. Also, his own life, and Dave's life, hung by a hair at that moment. Discovery of their presence would mean sudden death.

He heard Dave's voice. "Looks like they're headin' back to Sheep Springs." The cowboy spoke between rage-tightened lips. "The murderin' wolves."

The rustlers were moving slowly away, long shadows writhing like black, menacing shapes in their wake, and suddenly a low dip hid them from view.

Donal said curtly, "Let's take a look at that man."

They rode cautiously through the tall clumps of greasewood and dismounted near the sprawled body. Donal bent low for a closer look, muttered a startled exclamation.

"He's not dead!"

"Sure ain't," muttered Dave. "A dead man don't keep breathin' thataways."

They turned the senseless Monte over on his back with gentle hands. Dave whistled softly. "Gober's bullet nicked him in the head, creased him . . . knocked him cold." The cowboy grinned jubilantly. "I'll be doggoned—"

Donal nodded. "Lucky for him Gober didn't make sure," he said. He stood up, gazed down thoughtfully at the still form. "He didn't use good sense, telling Gober he was no cow thief, but it took nerve to do it . . . cold nerve. I like him for it, Dave, and I like his looks. It's my bet there's good stuff in this hombre."

"Nothing to do but wait for him to wake up," Donal decided. "Hate to lose the time, but we can't leave him." He felt in a pocket and fished out tobacco sack and papers. "Good thing they didn't bother to catch up his horse. See if you can get a rope over him, Dave."

Dave reached up to his saddle for the rope, halted the motion abruptly and gave Donal a startled look.

"Sounds like somebody yelled," he said uneasily.

They stood there, listening tensely, dismay in their eyes. The sound was unmistakable. The distant thud of hammering hoofs.

It was Donal's shrewd guess that a chance backward look had betrayed their presence, perhaps the flash of sunlight on gun metal, or the silver *conchas* that adorned Dave's leather chaps. The cause was of no importance now. The fact remained that some trifle had aroused doubts in Gober's mind.

Despite the anxiety that gripped him, his mind functioned coolly, seized upon the one chance. He knew Stormy's ability to run fast and far. The big black horse had no peer in the Rio Seco country.

"I'll lead them a chase away from here," he said to Dave. "Get back in the brush with your horse and keep out of sight. They don't know there are two of us. The moment I'm seen they'll ride hell bent on my tail." He flung himself into his saddle. "Listen, Dave—" He spoke sternly in a voice that denied argument. "Stay holed up out of sight until I've driven this pack of wolves a long way from here, then, the moment Monte can sit a saddle get him on his horse and head with him for the Devil's Hideout. There'll be a lookout posted there. Explain to Salty Wells and tell him to wait until I show up. Savvy?"

The cowboy nodded. He was already in his saddle, and with a parting gesture he vanished into the cover of the greasewood.

8

The black horse was running at top speed by the time the first of the returning rustlers appeared over the low rise a quarter of a mile away. A shout faintly touched Donal's ears. He glanced back, saw that the slope was suddenly alive with furiously riding horsemen. Gunsmoke flowered from hastily-fired rifles and he heard the vicious whine of bullets.

Satisfied that the rustlers had not seen Dave and that the angle of pursuit would clear the cowboy's hiding place by several hundred yards, he gave all his mind to the grim problem of out-running his pursuers.

It was rough country for fast riding, and presently the pursuers were forced to slacken speed. Donal took advantage of the respite to pull the black horse down to a fast running-walk, content to maintain the distance he had gained. Stormy could keep up that easy shuffling gait for hours and still be ready for a burst of speed when necessary.

Half an hour's riding brought him in sight of the railroad. A cattle train was moving slowly up the long grade from Cameron, and somewhat hazily at first a plan shaped in his mind. He had to make some use of that long string of cattle cars if he hoped to shake off pursuit. It was his shrewd guess that he had been recognized. Gober would make the most of the opportunity to even up the score. He would cling to the trail to the bitter end.

Donal thought briefly of Cameron. He might find friends there who would stand by. He discarded the idea. Gober would not hesitate to follow him. He had nearly a score of armed men. There was no safety in Cameron.

Again he concentrated on the approaching cattle train. It was an even chance he could manage the trick, and apparently the *one* chance to elude the men who sought his life.

He glanced back. The rustlers were spurring horses into a dead run. They were sure of him now. The train would block escape across the track. They would be on him before the track was cleared, and no matter which way he turned, they could cut him off. Already the approaching riders were spreading out to encircle him.

The locomotive, belching black smoke and cinders, loomed close. It was a matter of seconds now, and suddenly the black horse was racing across the track. Donal felt the engine's blistering heat on his face, and then the train was between him and his pursuers. For the moment the chase was blocked by the long string of rumbling cattle cars.

He slid from the saddle, gave the horse a slap

that sent him off in a startled gallop and then ran alongside the train creeping up the grade. Car after car slid past him as he sought for a handhold. Once he stumbled, recovered his footing and swung up to an empty flatcar.

He lay there, breathless, but jubilant. Gober was due for a surprise when he crossed the track. He would see the riderless horse and decide that Donal had sought cover in the brush, or perhaps had been wounded by one of their bullets and collapsed from his saddle. The rustlers would waste a lot of time, combing out every possible hiding place. He had no fear that they would catch the black horse. They would not get within yards of Stormy. The horse was wary of strangers and would find his way back to the ranch.

He sat up, felt in a pocket for cigarette paper and tobacco, his mind busy now on the problem of making his way to the Devil's Hideout where Salty Wells would be waiting for him. It would be folly to jump the train too soon. Gober was astute, might finally suspect the truth and post lookouts for him. His best plan was to leave the train at Latigo, a small cowtown some twenty miles east of Cameron. He knew old Ike Plester, who ran a livery barn there, and would have no trouble getting a horse.

He lit the cigarette and stared curiously at the loaded cattle car jolting in the wake of the flat. It was an open car with high sides built up with fence rails through which he could see the closely-packed steers.

Something drew his eyes like a magnet. He got to his feet, stood swaying for a moment to find his balance, then moved to the end of the flat for a closer look. The mark burned on the red hide pressed against the rails was unmistakably a Rocking D. He had known old Jim Daker's brand even before he could read. Those cattle were Ruth Merrill's steers.

From where he stood, Donal could look over the top of the loaded car. He counted three more similar cars, all of them packed with cattle. They comprised the tail-end of the long train.

He wondered about the caboose. Then suddenly he recalled noticing the caboose further up during his wild scramble along the track.

It required a few moments for the reason to dawn on him. The caboose was up front because the rear cars were to be dropped at Latigo and unloaded. It meant saving time in having to pick up the caboose again.

Donal stood there, swaying against the unsteady motion of the flat-car. He had learned enough from Alamo and Ruth to realize what had happened to old Jim Daker's Rocking D. His nephew and heir, murdered, Ruth herself a fugitive from her own ranch—from Anse Jasey and Al Gober. The answer was plain enough. Those Rocking D steers were being sneaked away to a distant range where in due time their brands would be altered. The wholesale stealing would never be discovered. It was a sure way of wrecking Ruth Merrill's inheritance.

He became aware that the train was increasing speed and realized they had topped the long grade. The cars jolted together, drew apart, jolted against each other again. An idea flared. He was familiar with this fifty mile spur his father had been instrumental in building. The road dipped for some five miles, then began another long upward climb. If he worked fast, watched his chance, he could uncouple the flat from the car in front. The train would pull away and the loss not be discovered until it had reached Latigo. He could easily brake the cars to a standstill once they struck the upgrade. All that remained would be to release the cattle, let them scatter into the chaparral.

There was danger in the plan if any of Gober's men were somewhere on the train. It was possible they would be in the caboose, but the fact that the shipment was coupled on for a quick drop indicated they would be in the tail-car with their horses. It was a risk he had to face, and at that he would have the advantage of surprise. A few moments could mean a lot.

He made his way to the front end of the flat-car and saw with relief that the coupling was of obsolete design, a heavy iron pin that could be drawn during one of the brief moments when the downgrade allowed the car to roll freely. A quick jerk before the slack was taken up again and the pin would slip out. Also the air-brakes were not hooked up, and for a good reason. These were old-type cars, used only for short hauls between Cameron and Latigo.

The engine hooted, smoke and cinders poured back, black and choking. Donal guessed that the fireman was stoking for the next long climb. He leaned over precariously and jerked at the big pin, sprawled back with it in his hands. In an instant he was on his feet and twisting hard on the hand brake.

Gradually the jolting wheels under him slowed, and as the impact of the upgrade came to his aid he saw a gap appear between the flat and the car in front. It widened swiftly; and the train vanished around a long bend.

Donal gave the hand brake a last twist and the cars jerked to a groaning standstill. Almost before the wheels stopped turning he was scrambling down. He ran to a clump of tall bushes that offered concealment, and waited, gun in hand.

Minutes passed. No sound broke the stillness. Donal began to think that after all the guardians of the cattle were enjoying the comforts of the caboose, now more than a mile away. He was about to step out from behind the bush when he heard a complaining voice from the end car.

“Seems like we’re standin’ here a hell of a long time,” grumbled the speaker. “Go take a look, Red.”

“Ain’t carin’ how long we sit here,” protested another voice. “I’m cravin’ to catch up on a lot of sleep these doggone cows have used up on us. Al Gober sure does work a man hard.”

A long silence, and Red’s aggrieved voice again. “Soon as we hit Latigo I’m makin’ tracks back to the Cimarron. Ain’t likin’ this Gober bunch and I ain’t trustin’ Gober. His face gives me the creeps. He’s a killer.”

Another silence, broken by the first speaker, his tone harsh. “Quit bellyachin’. Gober’s all right.”

“He’s a damn cow thief,” Red said, sullenly. “I got roped into this job before I savvied what was goin’ on at Rockin’ D. Me and Monte was both roped in. You know it’s the truth, Fargo.”

“Talkin’ won’t do you no good now,” replied Fargo, gruffly.

“Don’t you get hostile notions,” warned Red, his voice suddenly hard. “I’m jumpin’ this job soon as we hit Latigo, and you ain’t stoppin’ me.”

“Your *loco* talk makes me sick at the stummick,” grumbled Fargo. “I ain’t carin’ a hoot what you do. Wouldn’t be in *your* boots if you ever meet up with Gober ag’in.”

Donal heard the scrape of feet, then Red’s slow drawl, “Let’s take a look outside, Fargo. Beginnin’ to wonder my own self what’s holdin’ us here. Mebbe the engine's run off the track."

Booted feet thumped on the ground and the cowboys appeared from behind the car. They came to a frozen standstill, and stood staring with shocked, incredulous eyes.

The taller of the pair swore softly. He was long and lanky and his narrow face was covered with a stubble of red beard.

"Broke loose!" he exclaimed. "That's what she done, Fargo."

"Hell of a note," muttered Fargo. He was short and heavy set. Donal's gaze fastened on him as the more formidable of the two. He had restless, darting eyes in an expressionless dark face, a slow deliberateness about him that Donal guessed could be translated into lightning action.

Red rocked on his bootheels, showed a wide grin under his ropy red mustache. "Nothin' we can do till that train finds out she's dropped her tail," he chuckled. "Reckon I'll hunt me some shade and fill up on shuteye."

Fargo made no comment. He continued to stare up the track like a man pondering some weighty problem. His hand slid slowly and unobtrusively to the gun in his holster.

It was his misfortune that his own shadow betrayed that murderous intention. The lanky red-haired man glimpsed the swirling dark shape and sensed his danger. He flung himself sidewise. Even as he sprawled his length his own gun was out. Fargo, momentarily disconcerted by his miscalculation, lifted his gun for a second shot. Red's bullet took him between the eyes and without so much as a groan the would-be murderer crumpled to the ground.

Red got to his feet and stared dazedly at the dead man. Gradually, as he began to comprehend Fargo's perfidy, a look of bitter rage crept over his face.

"You low-down killin' wolf," he said aloud. "Kill me, huh? Leave me layin' in the chaparral some place for the buzzards to pick, huh?" He holstered the smoking gun and spat contemptuously. "Wasn't likin' what I said about Al Gober, huh? You doggone skunk!"

Donal studied him thoughtfully. The man had just narrowly escaped sudden death. He had killed the would-be assassin and his nerves were jumpy. It was more than probable that not even the threat of a gun in Donal's hand would prevent him from trying to shoot it out. He felt sorry for the man and hated the thought of being forced to kill him. He must think of some better way, and in a hurry. The cattle must be unloaded and scattered before the trainmen discovered the loss of the cars.

Donal sheathed his gun and moved away from the bush. "That was a close call, Red." His tone was casual, friendly.

The red-haired puncher spun on his heel, hand

reaching down to his gun. He halted the motion, stared at the tall man smiling at him.

Donal spoke again. "Don't blame you for killing him. I'd have done it myself, if you hadn't got him first."

Red found his tongue. "You seen it?" he asked.

Donal grinned, nodded. "I heard your talk back there in the car." His voice hardened. "I gather you're fed up with helping Al Gober steal cows."

The man eyed him doubtfully, and there was a hint of growing alarm in him, a menace in the spread-out fingers that hovered over the gun-butt.

Donal shook his head. "Don't try it, Red," he drawled. "You haven't a chance."

Red's hand relaxed. "You the law?"

"No. Not the law."

Red eyed him curiously. "You ain't Rockin' D. Never seen you over there."

"Not Rocking D," Donal said.

"Circle C, huh?"

"That's right," smiled Donal.

The red-haired cowboy jerked a nod at the cattle cars. "I reckon it was you that broke us loose from the train, huh?" There was admiration, a hint of awe in his voice.

"Right again," Donal said.

"You sure got plenty nerve," admired the cowboy. His face darkened. "What you figger to do with me?"

"Put you to work, unloading those steers,"

Donal told him crisply. He looked at the dead man. "We'll drag that body away, first," he added.

Red showed reluctance. "The skunk tried to kill me," he argued sulkily. "I'm for leavin' him where he lays."

"Those steers will trample him to a jelly," Donal said. "Come on, Red. Take hold of his legs."

"He figgered to leave me layin' in the chaparral some place," the cowboy said. "He was scared I'd talk too much, get the law on the trail of his cow-stealin' outfit. He figgered the train jaspers would soon be back to pick us up. He'd have gone off with 'em, left me layin' out yonder, and nobody knowin' he'd killed me."

"That's right," agreed Donal. His tone was curt. "You're a lucky man, Red, and if you've got good sense you'll pitch in and help. It's your chance to get back at Al Gober."

"Sure is." Red's face split in a wide grin. Without further protest he helped Donal drag the dead rustler behind a sheltering boulder.

They unloaded the horses, four of them. Two of them wore saddles. Red informed Donal that one of the saddled animals was his personal property.

"I'm headin' for the Cimarron," he said. He gave Donal a sly look.

"That's all right with me," Donal said. He

hesitated. "I picked up a friend of yours this morning," he added.

"Huh?" Red was mystified.

"Wears the name of Monte," Donal told him. "Gober shot him, left him for dead." He smiled grimly. "Gober didn't like his talk."

Red nodded solemnly. His face was pale. "Me and Monte sure acted *loco*, gettin' ourselves jobs with that outfit."

He shook his head dolefully. "I'd as soon herd sheep as go rustlin' cows."

"I believe you," Donal said.

"*Gracias.*" Red gave him an embarrassed grin, and they went to work unloading the cattle.

The steers poured through the side gates, taking the three-foot drop in frenzied leaps; in a few minutes they were stampeding into the chaparral which quickly swallowed them from view.

The two men hastily replaced the side gates, despite Red's protests that it was a waste of time.

Donal grinned at him. "We're building a mystery that will keep the railroad scratching its head for a long time," he said. "That train crew is going to be awfully puzzled when they get back to pick up their lost cars."

"Gober'll sure go ravin' crazy," chuckled Red.

"He won't dare say much," Donal prophesied. He looked speculatively at the cowboy. "Like a job with Circle C?"

Red shook his head. "I'm headin' a long ways

from the Rio Seco," he declared. "I ain't chancin' runnin' into Gober."

"Suit yourself," Donal said.

"I'm headin' back to the Cimarron." Red hesitated. "You can tell Monte," he added, an odd note of affection in his voice.

"I'll tell him," promised Donal. "One job more, Red." He gestured off at the dead man. "It will spoil the mystery if we leave him here."

In a few moments they had parted company, Donal on the dead rustler's horse and leading the spare horse on which was loaded Fargo's lifeless body. He rode south, following the direction taken by the stampeding cattle.

He was aware of a grim satisfaction when he thought of those steers. He had done a good job for Ruth Merrill, thanks to a chain of extraordinary circumstances. It was only the beginning, a first hard blow. Anse Jasey was going to learn he had blundered when he brought war to Circle C.

Two miles from the railroad track, he halted long enough to unload the dead rustler from the led horse which he turned loose to find its way to its own home corral. The animal wore an unfamiliar brand and was probably stolen from some distant ranch.

He was aware of an odd compassion as he covered the lifeless body with stones. The man was a thief and a killer. He had tried his best to shoot down an unsuspecting comrade. His kind were better dead, but he had been a human being, and could have been a brave and respected man instead of finishing life a renegade.

A sound broke the stillness there, a long drawn-out wail of a locomotive.

Donal grinned, swung up to his saddle. The trainmen were already hunting for their lost cattle cars. They were going to be very puzzled.

9

The bartender looked up from the big mail-order catalogue spread open before him, took one appraising glance at the man who pushed in through the swing doors and reached mechanically for a bottle from the array behind him. Another deft motion sent a glass spinning into the newcomer's ready hand. The hospitalities concluded, he resumed his leisurely study of the dog-eared catalogue.

"This small print is awful hard to read," he complained.

The customer reached for the bottle and critically eyed the label. "Mebbe you need specs," he said. He filled the glass and stood the bottle back on the bar. "You should get your eyes examined, Gus."

"Nothin' wrong with *my* eyes, Brasca." The bartender was inclined to be indignant. He was a paunchy man with a curved beak of a nose and sagging, mottled dewlaps that gave him the look of a turkey gobbler. "It's the tiny printin', and it don't help none, the way these pages get pawed over."

The Circle C man swallowed his drink, shuddered and put the glass down. "I reckon I need specs my own self," he said bitterly and frowned at the bottle. "I sure misread that label."

The barman looked at him suspiciously. "What's wrong with that there label?"

"I thought the printin' said *whiskey.*" Brasca shook his head sadly.

"It *is* whiskey." Gus glared at him.

"You mean it?" Brasca teetered on his high bootheels, a look of surprise on his leathery face. "Ain't it furniture polish, Gus?"

"No!" yelped the offended barman. He returned his attention to the catalogue.

Brasca grinned. "I'm takin' your word for it." He chuckled, reached for the bottle.

"Doggone you," grinned the mollified barman.

The Circle C man smacked his lips, put the glass down. "Sure *is* whiskey. That label wasn't lyin' none." He leaned against the bar conversationally. "What you huntin' up in that old Montgomery Ward book?"

"Nothin', special." Gus grinned sheepishly. "Kinda gives me a kick, lookin' it over and figgerin' what I'd buy me if I'd plenty *dinero.*"

Brasca nodded sympathetically. "A feller can get a awful spendin' itch, readin' that stuff," he said.

Gus sighed, closed the big catalogue, reached for his wet rag and made polishing motions on the bar. "What's keepin' you in town so long?" He leered knowingly. "A gal?"

"Huh?" Brasca's indignation was entirely fictitious. The barman's sly insinuation offered as good an excuse as any for his lingering in town. "Doggone your hide, Gus. Cain't a feller enjoy a rest in this cowtown without loose-minded hombres like you go to castin' evil 'spersions? Like the Bible says, 'Evil to him who evil thinks.' "

Gus stopped his polishing motions, frowned judicially and shook his head. "Seems like it was George Washington said them words the time folks claimed he cut down that cherry tree, or mebbe it was one of them royal kings a way back."

Brasca looked dubious. "That don't prove them words ain't fittin' you awful close," he maintained.

The barman guffawed, gestured at the bottle. "Have one on the house," he invited. "You sure give me a good laugh."

"*Gracias.*" The Circle C man shook his head. "I've l'arned not to use up my capacity all at one time." His friendly smile softened the refusal.

"Ain't a bad idee," agreed Gus.

"That's why I'm the man I am today," chuckled Brasca. He stroked his grizzled mustache complacently. "Waal, so-long, feller. Don't wear your eyes out on that catalogue." He turned leisurely toward the door, halted. "Speakin' of eyes, I reckon I'm sure needin' to go into specs my own self."

"Old age creepin' up on you, huh?" chuckled Gus.

"Sure was a joke on me," continued Brasca. "Seen the hombre comin' out of Romero's *cantina* over in Spanish town and thought he was Pasqual Torres. Give him a yell and when he turned it weren't him a-tall." He wagged his head sadly. "Hate to think my eyes is goin' back on me. The feller sure looked like Pasqual at that. Big hombre. Never seen him before." Brasca's tone took on speculative note. "Mebbe he was this Salvador Antista I've heard talk about."

The barman shook his head. "Wasn't him, if he was a big jasper. Antista is a little feller, kind of skinny and wears one of them tiny Mex mustaches."

"You know him, Gus?" Brasca's tone was casual.

"I've seen him around," admitted the barman. He was suddenly cautious, gave the cowboy a sly look. "Ain't seen him lately. I reckon he's left town."

"Mebbe so," drawled Brasca. His tone indicated complete indifference, and with a parting gesture he pushed through the swing doors.

He made his way slowly along the board sidewalk, hat tipped low against the glare of the sun. Despite his assumed role of an idler about town he was a very worried man. His search for Pasqual Torres had failed to turn up a single clue that would explain his disappearance.

Marica's admission that her son knew the mysterious Salvador Antista indicated that Pasqual might be involved in the plot against the ranch. An unpleasant thought that Brasca tried to down. He had been fond of Pasqual. It was hard to believe that a Circle C man would betray his old friends.

Brasca felt very low. His failure to pick up any definite news weighed heavily on him. The situation was too confusing. He liked action, enemies out in the open, guns blazing. He would know what to do, and no advice needed.

He failed to notice the cautiously peering face of the barman watching from the swing doors of the Longhorn Saloon. He was unaware that his apparently casual talk about Salvador Antista had hugely interested the barman.

Gus withdrew his turkey head from the door and meditatively rubbed his long beak of a nose. Suddenly he was tearing at the strings of his soiled apron.

"Pedro!" he called sharply. "Come pronto!"

A sleepy voice answered from a back room. "*Si*. W'at you wan'?"

"Keep an eye on the bar," Gus called back. "I've gotta go across the street to see a feller."

"*Si*, I come—" Feet shuffled up the back hall and an elderly Mexican slouched through the door.

Gus tossed his apron across the bar. “Be back in a few minutes,” he said. “Go easy on the likker, Pedro, or I’ll trim your ears for you.” He slammed hurriedly through the swing doors.

The old Mexican stood for a moment, an odd malevolence in his sunken eyes as he gazed at the gyrating doors. He fumbled under his belt, drew out a *machete* concealed in the leg of his baggy overalls and tentatively felt the keen edge with a forefinger. A grin broke the stolidity of his wrinkled brown face. It was an unpleasant grin; and replacing the wicked-looking knife he shuffled behind the bar.

Gus crossed the street, stopped to exchange greetings with a bearded rancher who was climbing into his wagon, and paused again in front of a new frame building squeezed between the Daker House and Luther’s Saddle and Harness Shop. It was a narrow, one story structure, painted a dazzling white and possessed the only real plate-glass window in San Benito. Neat gold leaf letters announced that it was occupied by

ANSON JASEY
ATTORNEY AT LAW
MINES • CATTLE

The saloon man hesitated, saw Sam Luther watching him from the doorway of his store.

"What's up, Gus?" The merchant's grin was sardonic, his eyes sharply inquisitive. "You come across the street like a bat out of hell."

Gus had reasons for not liking the lanky, satirical proprietor of the harness shop. Sam was a teetotaler, a leader of the minority group that frowned on the Longhorn Saloon & Dance Hall. Three recent shooting affairs had added to the tension.

"You're awful nosey," spluttered the saloon man. "Why don't you mind your own bus'ness?"

"Thought you was maybe runnin' for the marshal," grinned Sam. "Didn't hear no gunshots so maybe it was a stabbin' this time."

"Go to hell!" yelped Gus. With another sidelong glance at the lawyer's office door he continued on his way, climbed the hotel steps and pushed through the screen door into the lobby.

The clerk, a beefy-faced man in shirt sleeves, glanced up from a newspaper. "Hello, Gus."

Gus gave him a brief nod, went through another door and hurried along a narrow hall that led to the yard in the rear of the hotel. A Mexican girl sat on the kitchen steps, peeling potatoes which she dropped in a pan of water by her side. Gus paused, leered at her, made a grab at a smooth brown arm. The girl lifted her knife threateningly and with another leer he continued across the yard to the rear door of Jasey's office. The girl stuck out her tongue at his disappearing back.

Her name was Tulita Anda and she was Pedro's granddaughter.

She kept glancing over at the door through which Gus had disappeared. The motions of her paring knife grew slower and slower, and suddenly she got to her feet, picked up the pan of potatoes and ran up the steps. The kitchen door slammed shut behind her.

The three men in the lawyer's office looked at Gus inquiringly as he hesitated in the doorway. Anson Jasey was a slender, dark-haired man with quick bright eyes that gave him the wary look of a fox. He wore a small, pointed black mustache that lifted in a toothy smile as he looked at the saloon man.

"It's that Circle C hombre you told me to keep an eye on," Gus said. He stared with frank curiosity at the lawyer's two companions. "You fellers look like you'd been to hell and back," he added.

Al Gober gave him his mirthless grin. It was obvious that weariness and worry rode him heavily. "Sure have, Gus," he said. "Me and Ben both, huh, Ben?"

There was hostility in the look Ben Ferrel shot at the taller man. "We wouldn't be in this jam if we'd swung that jasper like I wanted," he said sulkily.

Al Gober regarded him intently. "Yeah?" His tone was ominously gentle. "Ain't you forgettin' it was you that let him bust loose?"

Ben squirmed visibly, lowered red-rimmed eyes. "My nerves is plumb frazzled," he complained. His look went to the bottle on Jasey's desk.

The lawyer nodded. "Help yourself, Ben." His voice was smooth, betrayed no hint of any perturbation. "It's all in the game—and the hand isn't played out—yet." His mustache lifted in his toothy smile. "What about the Circle C man, Gus?"

The saloon man smiled sourly. "He's smellin' round like an old wolf," he answered. "Tried to get me talkin' about Salvador Antista. He wasn't foolin' me none."

"What did you tell him?" asked Jasey.

"Told him Antista wasn't round here no more," grinned the saloon man. He shook his head. "Cain't tell about that Brasca hombre. He's smart."

Ben Ferrel replaced the bottle on the desk. "I'm feelin' peeved enough to go shoot it out with the skunk," he announced.

"Better order your coffin, first," sneered Gober. "You ain't got a lick of sense, Ben."

Ben started an annoyed rejoinder, subsided under Jasey's cold look. "Al is right, Ben," the lawyer said smoothly. "We can't go at this business bull-headed. We've got to use our brains." He stared thoughtfully at the saloon man.

"Thanks for the tip, Gus." He smiled. "Keep your ears open, and your mouth shut—about Antista."

Gus sensed that he was being dismissed. He retreated to the door, grinned back at the other men. "Drop over," he invited. "I'll set 'em up." The door closed behind him.

There was a long silence, broken by Jasey. "Your story doesn't sound possible," he grumbled. He drew a cigar from the pocket of his linen coat, bit off the end and applied a match. "Listens like a fairy tale." His sharp eyes probed them angrily. "You pick up young Cameron, take him over to Rocking D and stick him in the granary. Tied hand and foot. He gets loose and knocks Calico cold—leaves him hog-tied and goes off with Alamo and Ruth Merrill. We run into them up on the ridge road and Alamo kills Pete Starr."

An oath from Al Gober interrupted him. "Thought my skull was split clean open when that fool team r'ared back and upset the buckboard," he complained.

There was no sympathy in the look Jasey flung him. He continued, fingers tabulating on the desk. "Next thing, we find there's been a tip-off. We run into trouble at Sheep Springs." He looked hard at Gober. "You have an argument with Monte and kill him. But later you find his body has disappeared."

"That's right," Gober said. He shifted long legs uneasily, reached for the bottle.

"You claim you recognized Don Cameron and chased him clean to the railroad tracks—and then lost him."

"That's right." Gober replaced the bottle. "You ain't makin' a liar out of me, Anse."

"I'm merely pointing out the fairy tale elements," reminded Jasey acidly. "We hear of a mysterious accident to the train out of Cameron. The cars loaded with those Rocking D steers break loose. The trainmen discover the loss when they pull in to Latigo. They locate the lost cars, but the cars are empty, the side gates in place. No steers, no Fargo—no Red."

"It's spooky," muttered Ben Ferrel. "It just don't make sense."

Jasey shook his head at him. "No—" He spoke softly.

"It's Don Cameron, Ben. He's the spook that's been playing tag with you."

Gober broke his silence. "Plenty sign where them steers stampeded away from the cars," he said. "Scattered to hell and gone in the chaparral."

Jasey contemplated the cigar in his fingers, suddenly flung it into the cuspidor. "We'll show young Cameron a thing or two," he said in a thin, high voice.

"Have to work awful fast," Gober said sourly.

He glowered. "Where do you figger Alamo and the Merrill girl got to?"

"Only one place they'd go to," Jasey declared. He drew a fresh cigar from his pocket. "The Cameron ranch." He pushed the cigar back into his pocket with a fierce gesture. "I'm wondering how much Alamo knows about Colonel Merrill, and how much he's told Don Cameron."

"I don't savvy Alamo a-tall," grumbled Gober. "Don't make sense, him actin' like he done."

"I reckon the girl got him sorry for her," speculated Ben Ferrel. "Alamo was kind of soft about wimmen folk." He scowled. "I aim to get that old-timer for what he done to Pete Starr."

"That's all right with me," smiled Jasey. "Only remember one thing. None of these killings must point our way."

"Leave it to me," grinned the man. "He'll be found layin' in the brush, same as they found Rusty Cross."

"You're a cold-blooded devil," Jasey said.

"You should know." Ben's prominent eyes glinted wickedly. "You can't complain none about the *accident* that did for the Merrill girl's dad."

"I'm not so certain that Alamo hasn't guessed the truth," fretted Jasey.

"Guessin' ain't provin'," Gober said. He paused, eyes questioning the slender, dapper man behind the desk. "What's the next move, Anse?"

"Here's the situation—" Jasey spoke crisply. "We don't know how much Cameron suspects. He knows something is wrong, but he can't prove anything against you boys. Unless Alamo knows more than we think he does, Cameron has no reason to suspect *me.* I've been out to Circle C several times, had lunch with Cameron's mother. She regards me as a friend." Jasey touched his trim black mustache complacently. "A good-looking woman."

"She's a widder, Anse." Gober's long teeth showed in his mirthless smile. "She'll mebbe fall for a slick hombre like you."

"I'll keep it in mind," commented the lawyer. "She wouldn't be the first." His expression hardened. "It's like this, boys. I'm sitting pretty in this town. The rough stuff must be kept under cover. We're honest, respectable citizens and frown on such things as killings and cow-stealing."

"Won't be easy to fool Don Cameron," interrupted Gober. "Not after the way we laid for him in the trail."

"I'll take care of that," Jasey said. "I'll explain that it was all a mistake, a false rumor that led us to believe he was mixed up in the rustling that's going on in the Rio Seco."

"Sure will take some talkin' to do that," argued Gober.

"He'll listen," Jasey prophesied. "I've got a story rigged up for him."

"It's you that's the devil," muttered Ben Ferrel.

Jasey ignored him. "Watch your step when you're in town," he warned. "Don't start anything if you run into any of the Circle C bunch. They may be suspicious about that Sheep Springs business, but they have no proof against us."

"They got three of our men," reminded Gober.

"Killed them, you said, Ben." Jasey looked inquiringly at the stocky renegade. "You were there at the cabin, you said."

"Sure was," Ben swore feelingly. "We was fixin' to burn the place when that bunch jumped us from the piñon scrub. Their lead was buzzin' round us like hornets." Ben paused, a glassy look in his pale, bulging eyes. "Seen Stinger and Curly, layin' there, dead. Ain't sure what happened to Denny. Reckon he caught plenty of that lead."

Jasey stared at him, his expression ugly. "You're not sure about Denny—that he was killed?"

Ben shrugged. "I lit away from there awful fast," he said sourly. "I ain't knowin' for sure about Denny. He ain't showed up. It's my bet he's feedin' the buzzards by now."

"Won't be so good, if they took him alive." Jasey scowled, reached again for the cigar, chewed it reflectively. "We'll have to take a chance you're right about the buzzards."

Gober broke his silence. "I ain't carin' much for

this pussy-footin' play," he said gloomily. "You don't savvy this Circle C outfit like we does. Hell is goin' to bust right in our faces if we take 'em too easy."

"Done some bustin' already," grumbled Ben.

"If they're wise to our play I'd as soon tangle with a bunch of wildcats," Gober said. He got out of his chair. "Come on, Ben. Let's get goin'."

They pushed morosely through the door, into the warm afternoon sunshine of the back yard. Tulita, back on the kitchen steps with her pan of potatoes, gave them a sly look from lustrous dark eyes as they passed. Her gaze came back to the potato in her hand. She finished peeling it, dropped it with the others in the pan of water and rose with a single graceful motion to her feet.

Her look went again to the two men and as the screen door of the hotel hall slammed behind them, she sped swiftly down the steps and stooped to retrieve a potato that apparently had fallen from the open sack on the steps. She spoke softly in Spanish, mouth close to the wooden plank door of the closet under the steps.

"Quick, grandfather," she whispered. "They have gone. You must hasten to the señor—"

Tossing the recovered potato like a ball in her hand, she ran up the steps, reached for the pan and vanished into the kitchen.

10

The big store was the oldest building in San Benito. The thick adobe walls that rose shoulder high above the flat roof were pierced with loopholes. Old Angus Cameron was mindful of possible marauders when he established his trading post in that remote corner of the Territory of New Mexico.

A high log stockade had originally encircled the premises, but the section fronting on the main street had been removed. The rear portion now used as a corral was cut off from the street by a split-rail fence, laced with strands of barbed wire.

The original sign still hung from heavy iron hooks above the wide steps of the roomy porch that ran the full width of the building. Battered and weather-worn, it told the passer-by that the place was Cameron's Trading Post.

Old Angus was gone, and those who did not know the story would gaze with considerable astonishment at the dark-faced man who had succeeded to the prosperous business founded by the old Scotch trader and who wore the name of Roderick Dhu Cameron. Except for the slight burr in his voice, and the sterling honesty instilled in him by his dour old foster-father, there was no Scotch in Rod Cameron. He was a full-blooded

Apache, survivor of a massacre that had left him a helpless infant in his dead mother's arms. Pity, and a certain remorse, had impelled Angus to bring up the babe as his own son, and, save for the blood in him, Roderick Dhu was as Scottish as the grim old frontiersman who had given him his name and heritage.

He sat at the battered old desk in the rear of the long store, listening with tight-lipped attention to Donal. He was in his early forties, of medium height, a powerful, barrel-chested man.

"Ye mind me of the day your father came to the Post," he said. "I was but a lad and because we were both Camerons we became friends and brothers." A smile warmed his dark face. " 'Tis a friendship that the years have made stronger in me. There was trouble enough to give him the man's test in those days." Roderick Dhu shook his head solemnly. "Ay—disaster and death stalked him night and day, but the heart in him was Cameron and his courage like hard, bright steel."

"He used to tell me how Angus and you stood by," Donal said, his voice not quite steady.

"Camerons stick together," the trader said simply. His dark face took on a granite hardness. " 'Tis a verra serious business. I'm thinkin' Anse Jasey is at the bottom of it, though 'twill be har-rd to prove."

"We nabbed one of the gang at Sheep Springs,"

Donal told him. "That man keeps a shut mouth . . . won't talk."

The trader smiled bleakly. "I am bred to the ways of a Scot, but there are times when the customs of my mother's people can be useful." He shook his head regretfully. " 'Tis not a way old Angus considered righteous. I should not let the Apache in me speak of such things."

"I'm with Angus on that," Donal said. "The man may talk of his own free will in time. He knows there's a rope reaching for his neck, or a long term in prison, at the least."

" 'Tis har-rd to say." The trader's tone was dubious. "This Anse Jasey is an unscrupulous rascal—a clever lawyer." His face darkened. "The Rio Seco country has become a sanctuary for all the scoundrels of the border since this man came to San Benito. 'Tis said the new sheriff is his own jackal, and that is a bad thing and makes a mockery of the law."

Donal's face took on a grim, determined look. He said quietly, "My father brought law and order to the Rio Seco. You know that, Rod."

"Ay—with blazing guns," the older man said. His dark eyes gleamed.

"I'll do the same." Donal spoke grimly. "If Jasey has made a mockery of the law that rides with a sheriff, I'll give him his fill of an older law, the law of gun justice."

The trader leaned back in the creaky swivel

chair, an expression of huge content on his face. "Lad," he said affectionately, "I can hear your father say the verra same wor-rds. Ah, 'tis him ye are in body and spir-rit."

Pain stared at him from the younger man's eyes, and he added softly, "Ay, 'tis a great grief ye must bear, along with the wickedness and treachery of evil men, but bear it ye will, my brother. The clan Cameron is a fighting breed."

Donal was suddenly grinning, the weariness and worry gone from his face. "You darned old Highlander," he said affectionately. "We'll give 'em a taste of Cameron steel."

"Scots wha hae wi' Wallace bled." Roderick Dhu's eyes glowed. "Ay, that's the spir-rit!"

Brasca pushed in through a rear door. "Pedro Anda is out thar in the barn, Rod," he informed the trader. "He's scared to come into the store for fear he'll be seen."

"What does he want?" Roderick Dhu looked puzzled.

"Wasn't sayin'," answered the Circle C man. "Acts kind of scary—like the devil was on his tail."

The trader got out of his chair. "Back soon." He vanished through the door.

Brasca leaned against the desk, fingers busy with tobacco sack. "Cain't figger out where Pasqual has got to," he grumbled. "Don't look good."

Donal nodded. “I don’t like it,” he admitted.

The cowboy eyed him keenly. “Hate to think he’d pull off a low-down play on us.”

“Not Pasqual.” Donal spoke with conviction. “He wouldn’t go in for treachery. I know Pasqual.”

“Only one other answer.” Brasca wagged his head sadly. “He’s layin’ daid, some place.”

“Dead—or a prisoner,” Donal said.

Brasca lit his cigarette, scowled through the smoke. “I’ve an idee this town ain’t healthy for Circle C fellers.” He spoke grimly. “They’ll be layin’ for you, Don.”

“We have a few friends in San Benito,” reminded Donal.

“Sure.” Brasca was frankly dubious. “Thar’s Sam Luther, and Billy Winch. Billy is so old and crippled up he ain’t much help in a pinch.” He enumerated several more names on his fingers. “Close to a dozen, includin’ Rod.” He shook his head somberly. “Thar’s a lot of tough-lookin’ gents in this town, hang round the Longhorn come nights. I’d say they’d look a lot better dancin’ on air. Border scum . . . hang-tree fruit, that’s what they are.”

Donal grinned at him. Brasca was warning him to get out of town. The veteran Circle C man sensed his amusement.

“Yeah, I’m tellin’ you,” he growled. “You was a damn fool, comin’ here alone. Why didn’t you bring the outfit along?”

"Salty had to stay back at the camp with that shipment of steers," Donal reminded. "We're short-handed, Brasca."

"Could have fetched Dave along with you," Brasca said in an annoyed tone. "Dave's awful handy with his guns, you know. There's only two men in the outfit that's faster."

"Meaning that Bearcat and yourself are those two men," chuckled Donal.

"I ain't callin' you a liar," grinned the cowboy, "and I'm still claimin' you should have fetched Dave along. I'd sure like him sidin' us right now."

"I sent him back to the ranch with the man I told you about," explained Donal, patiently.

"That Monte hombre, huh!" Brasca squinted a thoughtful look at him. "You figger he's all right, boss?"

"I've put him on the payroll," Donal informed him. "Monte is a first-class man, Brasca. He got a wrong start with Gober's crowd. He's going to be valuable. You'll like him."

"Waal—" Brasca's tone was affectionate. "Thar's an awful lot of your dad in you, son, and your dad sure savvied men. Savvied 'em the way he savvied cows and I never knowed him to guess wrong no time, man or cows."

Donal was uncomfortably aware of disturbing doubts. Brasca was one of the old-timers, a survivor of the hard-bitten crew that had brought the first Circle C herd up from the Brazos. The old man was trying to comfort himself. He still lived in those stirring, gun-smoked days when he rode stirrup to stirrup with the old boss whose leadership never failed the outfit. The veteran Circle C man was determined to carry on the legend, make believe that in the son he saw the father.

Donal broke the brief silence. "*Gracias*. Living up to him is a big order, Brasca." His voice was husky with emotion.

Brasca seemed to understand. He said softly, "Me and Bearcat is ridin' herd with you, son, and we ain't frettin' none." He added grumblingly, "Sure wish Bearcat was here. Them guns he wears can talk mighty good."

"One reason why I told him to stick close to the house," Donal said. His eyes narrowed thoughtfully. "Anything can happen. That gang will be looking for Alamo—and Miss Merrill."

Brasca did not share his anxiety. "Bearcat and that Alamo feller are smart old-timers," he said. "I wouldn't get to worryin', boss." He paused, added fretfully, "It's *you* that's got me worried. This here town is crawlin' with wolves. Thar'll be plenty hell if they smell you out."

"I don't think Anse Jasey will start trouble in town," Donal argued. "He's a smooth article and likes to work under cover. He won't want to do anything that will damage his reputation here."

Brasca snorted skeptically. “He ain’t goin’ to set round doin’ nothing. Not after what you did to his outfit over to Sheep Springs.”

“He’s doing some hard thinking right now,” grinned Donal.

A saturnine grin spread over the cowboy’s leathery face. “You sure got the skunk scratchin’ his haid,” he chortled. “At that it won’t take him long to add up two and two and get the right answer about them cattle cars you broke loose from the train. Sounds like Rod comin’ back,” he added.

The trader pushed in through the back door, paused briefly to scrutinize two men entering the store from the street. A clerk stepped toward them inquiringly, and one of the men gestured at a pile of saddle blankets on the counter.

Something in the trader’s manner telegraphed a warning to Brasca. He swung his lean frame from the desk and leaned against the wall in a position that gave him a full view down the long store. He stood there, bleak eyes covertly watching the customers now examining the saddle blankets. They were a hard-looking pair, and, from their sly glances, obviously as much interested in the little group at the desk as they were in the blankets.

Roderick Dhu resumed his seat in the swivel chair and gave Donal a grim smile. The glitter in his eyes betrayed excitement. His look slid past Donal to the pair at the blanket counter.

He said softly, "Spies . . . Jasey's on your trail."

"They won't start anything in here," Donal said.

"I half wish they would." The Apache's brown fingers hovered longingly over the gun in the drawer.

The wrangling voices grew louder. "These blankets ain't worth a damn," one of the customers grumbled. "Hell! We're wastin' our time lookin' at 'em."

The trader got to his feet, angry gaze fixed on the bogus customers. "You bums get out of this store," he said. "We don't want your trade."

The man's head turned in a contemptuous stare. "I ain't takin' no back talk from no Injun," he sneered. "You go to hell, feller." He stood spraddle-legged, hand on gun-butt, lips twisted in a vicious snarl.

The trader's hand dropped to the drawer, came up with the gun. "Get out!" His voice was a whiplash, and the bite of it seemed to put caution in the man. He darted an appraising look at Brasca, met his cold, unwinking stare. His bravado faded. He muttered something to his companion and backed toward the door.

"I ain't startin' nothin'—" There was a hint of panic in his sullen voice.

"Tell your boss I've no use for spies in my store," the Apache said harshly.

The only answer was the hurried clatter of their

booted feet as they fled down the porch steps. The trader's taut expression relaxed, and grinning at the other men he resumed his seat and dropped the gun back into the drawer.

"Border scum," he grunted. "They couldn't fool anybody."

"Them fellers ain't carin' for a even break," Brasca said contemptuously. "They're pizen rattlers that like to lay in the grass and get you when you ain't lookin'." His eyes narrowed thoughtfully. "I'm insultin' honest rattlers with them words. A rattler gives warnin', which same their breed of snakes don't."

"That's right," agreed Donal. His eyes questioned the trader. "You picked up some news from Pedro Anda?"

Roderick Dhu nodded, fingers busy tamping tobacco in a pipe. "Pedro works at the Longhorn," he said. "He's in a way to pick up a lot of gossip. Most of it is none of his business. Right now he's a worried old man. You can maybe guess why."

"Something about Pasqual Torres," ventured Donal.

Brasca said bitterly, "Doggone—I sure overlooked a bet in that Mex hombre."

"It seems that Pasqual is sweet on old Pedro's granddaughter, Tulita. She works over at the Daker House, and she's been hearing talk, too, and using her eyes." The Scot's burr in the Apache's voice was a breath from the Highlands of his beloved foster-father. "A verra smar-rt lass," he chuckled.

"Purty as a pitcher," declared Brasca. "Don't blame Pasqual a-tall for goin' soft on her." A vast relief was in the old cowboy's eyes. Pasqual was not a traitor, nor was he a corpse, "laying out in the chaparral" to feed the buzzards.

He voiced his hopes: "Meanin' you got news of him, Rod?"

Roderick Dhu nodded. "Pedro saw him in the Longhorn day before yesterday. He was drinking with another Mexican whose name he does not know. The two were sitting at one of the tables and Pedro says they talked a lot, kind of secret, kept their voices low. Gus, the barman, kept taking them drinks which they would empty in the cuspidor when he wasn't looking. Pedro was interested in Pasqual because of Tulita, which was why he happened to see Anse Jasey join them at the table. He says that Jasey was very friendly with them, called for drinks which Gus served them. Jasey's drink was in a long-stemmed glass and apparently was wine. The other two glasses contained whiskey which Pasqual and his Mexican friend immediately drank. Jasey chatted with them for a few minutes and then left the saloon."

Donal and Brasca exchanged grim looks. The trader nodded. "Yes," he said. "You've guessed it. Pedro says that soon after Jasey left he saw Gus go over to the table where Pasqual and his friend seemed to be in a drunken stupor. Gus did some cursing, called Pedro over to help him carry the men into a back room to sleep it off. Pedro was busy for the next hour or so, he says, and when he went back for a look he found that Pasqual and his Mexican friend had disappeared."

"The unknown Mexican was Salvador Antista," guessed Donal.

The trader nodded. "That's what Pedro claims, now. He learned it from Tulita. She's been keeping her ears and eyes open. It seems that Jasey has a lot of visitors who use his back door. They go through the hotel and reach the door by way of the yard. Tulita was suspicious and gave old Pedro the tip, hid him under the kitchen steps. He picked up some news that explains the disappearance of Pasqual and Antista."

"He knows where they are?" Donal asked.

The trader shook his head gloomily. "Somewhere in town, Pedro thinks. He is an old man and has not the wits to cope with the business. Tulita sent him to me with the story."

"I'll have a talk with the girl," Donal decided.

Brasca slapped a hard hand on the desk. "I'm for headin' over to Jasey's office and stickin' a gun in his belly." He spoke in a tight, furious voice. "Make him come clean about Pasqual."

"He'd laugh at us," Donal said. He shook his head. "We've got to work out a better plan,

Brasca. He's smart, and we've got to be smarter." He got out of his chair, looked thoughtfully at the cowboy. "See if you can get in touch with Pedro and fix up some way for us to have a talk with Tulita."

"Sure." Brasca nodded. "I'll mosey over to the Longhorn right now." He hesitated, looked at Donal suspiciously. "You figger to stay here in the store till I get back?"

"I'm going to have a little chat with Jasey," Donal told him.

"You make me sick," fumed the old cowboy.

"He won't try any rough stuff," Donal said.

Brasca glowered. "I'm goin' with you," he insisted doggedly. "I ain't trustin' you alone in this town."

"Jasey would take one look at that face of yours and reach for a gun." Donal grinned. "You look too belligerent."

"I'm feelin' that way," muttered the cowboy.

"That's why I don't want you along." A chill note crept in the young Circle C man's voice. "You go hunt up Pedro Anda and leave Jasey to me."

Brasca's eyes narrowed in a keen look at him, and something like wonder spread over his grim face. "Talk the way your dad used to when we tried to buck him." He laughed softly, the gloom gone from him. "See you later, boss." He threw the trader a grin and headed for the door.

Roderick Dhu stared up thoughtfully at his young friend. "I'm thinking that Brasca is right," he worried. "This Jasey is a verra dangerous man."

"I'm not afraid of him," Donal said.

Roderick Dhu gave him a look of mingled affection and pride. "A Cameron is no afraid of man or devil. Ay, my brother, 'tis a truth that old Angus bred in me, and the same truth is in you from the brave man whose name ye bear." He stood up, clapped a hand on the younger man's shoulder. "I'll no say ye are wr-rong in your pairpose."

Left alone, the swarthy trader wandered restlessly around the big store, gave brusque orders to the clerks, waited on a Navajo squaw who came in with a rug under one arm. She chose a bolt of bright red silk, and after a little bargaining paid for it with the Navajo rug and a pair of silver bracelets that she slipped from a slim brown wrist. She seemed a bit surprised at the liberal exchange, gave him a shy little smile and hastily left before he should demand the other pair of bracelets she had been prepared to give him.

The Apache's gaze followed her, remained fixed abstractedly on the sunlit street beyond the door. He was well aware that he had cheated himself, but for the moment his trader's instincts were sadly out of gear. His thoughts were with young Donal Cameron and he was aware of disturbing misgivings.

He went slowly back to his desk and after a moment's scowling indecision jerked the top drawer open, reached for the gun and slipped it in the shoulder-holster concealed under his coat.

"Ye'll mind the store while I'm gone," he said to his assistant. And remembering his recent and unprofitable transaction with the young squaw, he added grimly, "Ye'll no forget to watch the pr-rices, Mister Carson. We can no afford to give our goods away." He stalked out of the store, whistling softly and keeping step to the tune.

Mr. Carson, a thin, stoop-shouldered man, gazed after him shrewdly. He was not Scotch himself, but he was familiar with that tune the boss was whistling. Something about the Campbells coming. It was a tune the boss always whistled when worry rode him.

Mr. Carson wagged his head gloomily. Something was indeed wrong, or the boss wouldn't practically have made a present of that silk to the squaw. It wasn't like the boss to forget his profit.

11

The street drowsed under the fierce glare of the midday sun. The last vestige of mud had crumbled to dust that riffled lazily in the wake of the three horsemen riding slowly up the street from Billy Winch's livery barn.

Something familiar about the tall, gaunt man on the roan horse drew Donal's eyes like a magnet. He halted abruptly, stood tense and watchful, hand on holstered gun.

The roan's rider spoke softly to his companions and the trio reined their horses and looked at the man on the sidewalk.

"I'd like a word with you, Gober," Donal said.

Gober's grin indicated polite surprise. "What is it you want, stranger?"

"I'm no stranger to you," Donal said acidly.

The man was something of an actor. Astonishment spread over the bony mask of his face, a hint of embarrassment. "Sure, sure—" His tone was apologetic. "Mighty glad to meet up with you ag'in, Cameron. Wasn't knowin' you right off." He slumped forward in his customary easy slouch. "Looks like Ben and me made a mistake about you back there on the trail the other morning."

"Are you sure it was a mistake?"

"Don't blame you for feelin' some upset," smiled Gober. "A lot of cow-stealin' going on in these parts. Seems like the gang is bossed by a feller that claims the same name you wear. You cain't blame us for nabbin' you the way we done."

"Makes a good story." Donal's eyes narrowed watchfully. "Tell your friends to keep their hands off their guns," he advised. "I'm not taking chances with you, Gober."

Gober looked at him reproachfully. "We ain't looking for trouble with *you,* now we know you ain't the man we figgered you was."

"You talked about Circle C," Donal reminded him. "You talked about my father. You're not fooling me with your story."

"You're all wrong," Gober declared earnestly. "Ben and me was trying to trip you up with our talk about Circle C." He gestured. "That's why I wouldn't let Ben swing you like he wanted. The way you talked got me to thinkin' that mebbe you *was* the real Don Cameron and not the cow thief we figgered. That's why I told Ben to keep you locked up and headed for town to get Anse Jasey over. It's the howlin' truth. You ask Anse Jasey."

"I'll do that," Donal said coldly.

Gober grinned. "Him and you will get along fine," he prophesied. "Well, so long, Cameron. No hard feelin's, huh?"

Donal watched as they jogged on up the street.

He guessed from the direction they were taking that Gober was returning to the Daker ranch.

His expression thoughtful, he continued along the planked sidewalk. He was deeply suspicious of Gober's apparent friendliness, his protestations. The man's trumped-up story was proof that Jasey was spinning a new and more deadly web. In the meantime, orders had gone out to take things easy, until the stage was set for the final and devastating blow.

The wide, dusty street was awakening from its forenoon lethargy. Ranch wagons and buckboards were tying up at the long hitch-rails. Cowboys drifted up the street and off-saddled in front of the Longhorn Saloon, or left their horses in the shade of the big cottonwood trees that clustered around the Daker House. Old Jim Daker had planted them when he built the hotel more than twenty years earlier. The sight of those great spreading branches sent a twinge of pain through Donal. The bluff old cattleman would turn in his grave if he could know of the grim events that were wrecking the vast ranch his indomitable courage had wrested from a hostile wilderness, and bringing shame to the little town he had helped develop from the days when Angus Cameron's trading post was the one and only building.

A voice hailed him, and he saw Sam Luther, standing in the entrance of his harness shop. He crossed over, stood grinning, and returning Sam's handshake.

"Brasca was telling me you got back," Sam said, and he added in a low voice, "Was mighty sorry to hear about your dad."

Donal said, "It's tough, Sam—you know that."

Sam nodded, and sensing the grief was still a raw wound, he tactfully changed the subject. "This cowtown is going to hell fast," he grumbled. "Old Jim Daker would throw a fit if he could see the place. Nothing but a robber's roost, that's San Benito today. I've a notion to pull up stakes."

Donal stared at him. "I wouldn't do that, Sam," he said soberly.

The harness man reddened. He sensed a sting in the soft-spoken words. "My God, Don—I don't scare easy. I can take as much as the next man." He gestured helplessly. "It's the damn uncertainty. We've got no law here no more, since this Jasey feller come. He's got his fingers on the throat of this town and he's choking the life out of her."

"I've been hearing a lot about him," Donal said. "None of it good."

"He's slick," Sam told him bitterly. He studied the younger man shrewdly. "You aim to lock horns with him, Don?"

Donal nodded. "That's why I'm telling you to drop that notion of pulling up stakes."

"He's slick," repeated Sam.

"It's up to us to outsmart him," Donal said.

A tall, heavy-shouldered man emerged from the lobby of the Daker House. Sam Luther said in a low voice, "That's Bittner. Watch out for him, Don."

"Who's Bittner?"

"The new sheriff, and I'm telling you right now that Jasey owns him lock, stock and barrel."

The big man tramped heavily down the hotel porch steps and paused in front of Jasey's plate-glass front. Donal was aware of small red-rimmed eyes scrutinizing him suspiciously. There was the ugly menace of an angry bull in that lowering face.

"Hello, Sam." The sheriff drew a cigar from his vest pocket. "Who's your friend?" He chewed at the end of the cigar, spat out fragments of tobacco. "Like to get acquainted with folks in my bailiwick," he added with what was intended for a friendly grin.

"Meet Don Cameron," introduced Sam. "Don, this is Cal Bittner, our new sheriff."

"Cameron, huh?" Sheriff Bittner's beefy red face hardened perceptibly. "Meanin' Circle C?"

"That's right." Donal studied the man with cool, questioning eyes. "Newcomer in the Rio Seco, aren't you?"

"Been here close on a year," the sheriff answered. "Bought the old Aker spread south of Tule Creek."

"That's news." Donal frowned. "Hadn't heard that Bill Aker had sold out."

"Bill's dead," Sam Luther broke in. He gave Donal an unhappy look. "Him and his kid had a run-in with a bunch of rustlers. Rusty Cross found 'em layin' dead in the yard."

"I'm awfully behind on the news," Donal admitted grimly. "Poor old Bill!"

"I aim to put a stop to this damn lawlessness," Sheriff Bittner announced blusteringly.

"A good idea," Donal said with a thin smile. "Glad to have met you, Sheriff." He moved leisurely toward Jasey's office door, came to a frozen standstill as he felt the prod of hard metal against his spine, heard Bittner's gruff, exultant voice.

"I'm beginnin' on you, Cameron," the sheriff said. "I'm throwin' you in jail."

Donal slowly turned his head in a look at him. "What for, Bittner?"

"Take it easy," warned the sheriff. "I've got a warrant, all legal, for your arrest. I'm squeezin' this trigger if you get funny notions."

Donal heard Sam Luther's shocked voice. "Look here, Sheriff. You can't do this to Don Cameron. You're crazy!"

Two men hurried across the street from a group lounging in front of the saloon. They drew their guns and menaced the quickly-gathering crowd.

"Get movin', feller." Bittner's voice was loud,

arrogant, obviously intended to be heard by the bystanders. "You ain't gettin' help from nobody."

Donal repeated his question. "I've a right to know what the charge is," he said.

"Kidnappin'," the sheriff told him gruffly.

"You're crazy," Donal said. Unpleasant prickles chased up and down his spine. He had underestimated Anse Jasey.

Bittner continued with further details. "There's more to it than that," he said zestfully. "The charge includes aidin' and abettin' a murderer to escape justice and otherwise plottin' ag'in the peace."

A glimmer of the truth came to Donal. He said quietly, "It's a frame-up, Sheriff. You're only heading into a lot of trouble. Who signed this complaint?"

"I ain't talkin' about it here in the street," Bittner said irritably. "Get movin', Cameron. You can talk all you want in jail."

There was no arguing against the gun that prodded viciously into his back. Donal reluctantly obeyed. Bittner and the deputies followed close on his heels.

They were halfway across the street when a commotion in the saloon brought them to an abrupt halt. Donal heard Brasca's loud and profane voice, the swing doors flew open and the impact of several struggling men. It was over in a moment, with Brasca firmly gripped by three pairs of hands and gasping bitter curses.

"He was fixin' to pull his gun on you, Sheriff," one of the men said, breathlessly. He wiped blood from a cut lip. "He sure is one fightin' grizzly. Took three of us to gentle him."

"Don't act none too gentle yet," chortled the sheriff. "Who in hell is this hombre?"

"He's a Circle C feller," a voice answered.

Brasca twisted his head for a look at the speaker, framed in the saloon entrance. "You're a low-down skunk, Gus." He spat the words. "A double-crossin', crawlin' snake."

"Shut up!" bellowed the sheriff. "I'm jailin' you for disturbin' the peace of this town, and—" He flung Donal a malicious grin, "and for attemptin' to obstruct the law."

Brasca was beside himself with rage. "You damn fake sheriff!" he bawled. "You ain't puttin' Don Cameron in no jail."

"You and him both," grinned Bittner. "All right, boys. Bring that grizzly along. We'll fix him up with a nice cage he won't bust loose from in a hurry."

Donal heard Roderick Dhu's voice. "A wor-rd with ye, Bittner—"

The sheriff hesitated, looked at the Apache uneasily. "Yeah?" There was a hint of deference in his blustering voice. "I'm busy right now, Mr. Cameron."

"Ay, and 'tis business ye'd do well to drop,

I'm thinkin'." The trader's burred voice was ominously gentle. "A new man to these parts ye are, Bittner, or ye'd no lay hands on Donal Cameron."

"I ain't takin' orders from you," fumed Bittner.

"Ye'll no take him to jail," the trader said calmly.

The sheriff blinked at him. It was plain that he had a wholesome respect for the Apache. He stood there, glowering, gun dangling in lowered hand.

Donal saw the indecision in him. His hand moved swiftly, jerked his confiscated gun from the sheriff's holster. Bittner let out a startled grunt, stared down, slack-jawed, at the gun menacing his belly. A shudder ran through him and his red, perspiring face took on a sickly green tinge. The .45 slipped from his limp fingers, fell with a soft thud on the ground.

Donal flashed a look at the shocked deputies. "Take it easy," he warned.

The deputies exchanged dismayed looks and slowly pushed their guns into holsters.

"Seems like you fellers have lost the deal," cackled Brasca.

"Sure have," grunted one of the deputies. He turned on his heel.

"Just one little moment, kind sir." The old Circle C man's voice dripped honeyed politeness. "Ain't you forgettin' somethin'?"

The deputy halted, scowled back at him. "Ain't I said we've throwed in our hands?"

Brasca waddled toward him. "You ain't needin' that ace card of mine you've got in your belt," he chuckled.

The deputy grinned sheepishly. "Sure, sure. I get you." He drew Brasca's gun from his belt and handed it to the cowboy.

"Thank you so kindly," grinned Brasca. He balanced the long-barreled Colt in his big-fisted hand. "Now you two sidewinders get to hell out of here," he added in a hard, rasping voice. "My polite nature is goin' sour on me awful fast."

The deputy's look slid past him to the sheriff. Something he read in Bittner's furious eyes seemed to impress him. He gave Brasca a sour smile.

"No call to worry no more about me, pardner," he said. "I'm forkin' my bronc right now and headin' a long ways from this cowtown."

"Me, too," muttered the other deputy. He hurriedly followed his companion.

Donal smiled acidly at the sheriff. "Your deputies don't like their jobs, Bittner," he commented.

The sheriff licked dry lips. "You're headin' for plenty trouble, Cameron," he said thickly. "Buckin' the law."

Roderick Dhu said mildly, "I warned you to keep your hands off him, Bittner."

"If you'd kept your nose out of it I'd have had him in jail by now."

"I hae me doots," chuckled the trader. " 'Tis plain ye dinna ken the Cameron breed."

"You took my mind off him," grumbled the sheriff.

"He was only needing that one little second of distraction," smiled the Apache.

"You helped him resist arrest," Bittner said savagely. "You ain't heard the last of this business." He gave Donal a sly look and reached down for his fallen revolver.

Donal offered no protest, but as the sheriff turned to leave them he said quietly, "Just a moment, Bittner. I'd like to see that warrant for my arrest."

Bittner halted, looked back at him. "You'll be seein' it soon enough, feller." His lips twisted in an ugly grin.

"I'm seeing it *now,*" Donal said.

Bittner hesitated, glanced desperately at Jasey's office door. He had the look of a man hopelessly trapped. His hand slid suspiciously close to the gun he had replaced in its holster.

Donal shook his head warningly. "Don't try it." His own glance flickered across the street at the lawyer's plate-glass front, glimpsed a tell-tale shadow. He smiled bleakly at the harassed sheriff. "You're a liar," he said. "You have no warrant in your pocket. Isn't that the truth, Bittner?"

Bittner wiped his red, perspiring face. He said huskily, "Ain't got 'em on me . . . sure, that's right."

Donal pressed him, his voice a whiplash. "There is no warrant. Isn't that right?"

Bittner nodded. "Yeah, that's right," he admitted sullenly.

Donal's hand reached out, grasped his arm. "Who's back of the frame-up? Don't stall, Bittner."

"I've done talkin'," muttered the sheriff. "Let loose of me, feller." His voice rose blusteringly. "I'm the law in this town."

"You're a cheap crook," Donal told him. His balled fist lashed out.

The blow sent the sheriff reeling. He recovered his balance, wiped his bleeding nose and charged the Circle C man, head lowered, arms swinging.

Donal side-stepped the rush and swung stinging rights and lefts to the big man's face that left his mouth a red smear.

Bittner had no will to take the punishment. He backed away, hands covering his face. "I'm quittin'," he gasped. "Damn you, I'm quittin'."

"I'm asking you that question again," Donal said. "Who's back of this frame-up?"

The sheriff groaned. "I'm turnin' in my star," he said despairingly. "I'm ruined in this town. I'll be dead meat."

"You're answering that question first," Donal said grimly.

Bittner looked at him with fear-filled eyes. "He'll kill me—" He spoke hoarsely.

"Who'll kill you?" asked Donal.

"Anse Jasey."

"Is he the man you take orders from?"

"Yeah—" Bittner's eyes rolled in a terrified look at the lawyer's office. "He's a devil, Cameron. I'm tellin' you!"

"He got you elected sheriff to do his dirty work?"

Bittner nodded, wiped his hot, bleeding face with his shirt sleeve. "I reckon that's it."

" 'Twas a fraudulent election, I'm thinkin'," Roderick Dhu said gravely. "There's already talk of an investigation." He shook his head gloomily. " 'Tis easy for crooks to get control when honest men take no interest in county affairs."

"What this county needs is a few necktie parties," grumbled Brasca. He eyed Bittner's quivering bulk longingly. "I'm for startin' in on this hombre. He'd look pretty, danglin' from one of them cottonwoods in front of the Daker House."

Donal grinned. "He'll be no use to us dead, Brasca." He paused, stared thoughtfully at Bittner. "Let's see that sheriff's star you wear." He held out a hand.

Bittner unfastened the badge with shaky fingers. "I ain't needin' it," he muttered.

Donal dropped the badge into a pocket. "You've turned in your star," he announced. "You've resigned your sheriff job in front of witnesses, and now you're going for a ride with us, Bittner." He looked at Brasca. "Take his gun," he said.

"You've got me guessin', son." Brasca grinned at the dazed Bittner. "Excuse me, kind sir—" He plucked the gun from Bittner's holster. "A right nice weepon."

The ex-sheriff said bitterly, "What the hell—"

"You'll be a lot safer at Circle C than running round loose," Donal explained. He gave Brasca a nod. "Take him over to the Trading Post corral and wait for me."

Brasca eyed him suspiciously. "Ain't you done enough for one day?"

"I'm wanting that little talk with Anse Jasey," Donal said. He glanced at the office door. "I've an idea he's been watching our argument with his sheriff."

"You sure do go lookin' for trouble," mourned Brasca.

"I'm looking for Pasqual Torres," Donal reminded gently. "I think our friend Jasey can tell me about Pasqual, and about some other things I want to know."

12

He was surprised to find the lawyer's office door locked. He knocked, listened intently for some sound, and then he saw the card clipped to the shade pulled down over the plate glass. The large block letters formed three brief words, OUT OF TOWN.

Donal stared with disbelieving eyes. He was sure that he had seen Jasey at the window, a fleeting glimpse of his moving shadow silhouetted on the drawn shade.

Anger grew in him as he stared at the card. It was a trick. Jasey was determined to avoid a meeting and had sought refuge behind locked doors. The collapse of his plan to jail Donal, the humiliation of his sheriff, must have alarmed the scheming lawyer. He wanted time to think it over.

Donal's look went thoughtfully to the wide, shady porch of the Daker House. He was recalling what the Mexican girl had said about the back door which could be reached by way of the hotel lobby.

He climbed the porch steps leisurely, paused to light a cigarette. Any show of hurry might betray his purpose to prying eyes. The brief episode with the sheriff had caused plenty of excitement. He sensed that his every move was under watchful scrutiny.

Disturbing doubts assailed him as his gaze slid from group to group. There were faces he knew—old friends. Not one of them had raised a protesting voice when Bittner had rammed a gun into his back. Only Roderick Dhu possessed the courage to speak his mind. Something was very wrong when honest men feared to take a stand.

It came to him that history was repeating itself. The Rio Seco had reverted to the old lawless days when fear stalked the range, and murder lurked in every mesquite bush. Any honest cowman was a potential victim of the organized gang of rustlers that had swarmed in like ravening wolves. Fear of grisly reprisals made men look the other way, kept their mouths shut. It was fear that made men weak.

Implacable purpose grew in Donal as he recalled the grim saga of those long-gone days when Circle C had waged war against the human wolves who lived by bloodshed and pillage. Under his father's leadership, fear-ridden cow-men had rallied wavering courage and joined in the bitter fight. Law had replaced lawlessness, and men no longer rode in fear of an unseen assassin's bullet.

The answer was there for him to read in those unwritten pages of range history. Leadership that would weld honest men into a compact force for law and order, forge an irresistible weapon against the dark command of evil minds.

The screen door at his back opened and slammed shut and a man hastily emerged from the lobby. He was slim and wiry and wore the dusty garb common to the range. Donal glimpsed a dark face under shadowing hat brim, a smudge of black mustache, and a pair of sharp eyes that threw him a careless glance as he passed on down the porch steps.

Donal's gaze followed him curiously. He had never seen the man before. He had the look of an exceptionally able ranch foreman or top-hand.

A vague uneasiness stirred in him as he watched. He had the uncomfortable feeling that he was looking at a picture and seeing it all wrong.

The stranger slipped the tie-rope of one of the horses under the shade of the cottonwoods, swung effortlessly into the saddle and rode down the street.

Two men lounging near the horses that drooped at the hitch-rail in front of the Longhorn Saloon exchanged brief glances, slid into their saddles and rode leisurely in the same direction.

A suspicion of the truth spun Donal round to the screen door. The picture was beginning to make sense. He pushed into the lobby and made for the door that led to the rear hall.

The beefy-faced clerk jerked out of his chair.

"Where you goin', feller?" His tone of voice was belligerent.

Donal stared back at him. "I'm looking for Jasey," he said. "Any objection?"

The clerk eyed him suspiciously, fingers brushing at an enormous handle-bar mustache that had the gloss of black patent leather. "Nary a damn objection." There was a hint of malicious satisfaction in his grin. "Only one trouble about it, feller. He ain't in his office. Might as well save your feet a walk down that hall."

"I'm taking a look," Donal said curtly. He slammed through the door and ran down the dark passage.

He had the impression of a face watching through the screen as he hurried past the hotel kitchen. The glint of black hair hinted at Tulita. He hoped that his guess was right. He would want to question her.

As he suspected, the back door of Jasey's office was locked. The clerk had told the truth. The lawyer was not in his office.

Smarting at his failure to guess the identity of the man who had so coolly passed him on the hotel porch and ridden away, Donal turned disconsolately from the door. Jasey had tricked him nicely. In a way, the advantage had been Jasey's. Donal had never seen him, nor had he been given a description of the lawyer's looks. Only that he wore the tailored clothes of a city man and was something of a dandy. The dusty cowman's garb, the rasping spurs, the battered wide-brimmed hat, made an effectual disguise.

Again Donal glimpsed the pale oval of the girl's face behind the kitchen screen door. He halted close to the steps.

She came out timidly, stood on the top step, her eyes shy and big with mingled excitement and anxiety. She was a pretty girl, with blue-black hair parted in the middle and swept back over the ears. The effect was pleasingly madonna-like. Donal found himself appreciating Pasqual Torres' interest in her.

He said, "You know me, Tulita?"

"*Si, señor.*" She nodded her dark head, smiled shyly. "Pasqual have talk of you. He said you mooch long way in Cuba, weeth old senior."

"Pasqual does not know I'm back," Donal said. "How do you know I'm Donal Cameron? You've never seen me before."

She came down the steps, stood close to him. "I 'ave seen old señor." She smiled faintly. "I see you 'ave fight with that *malo hombre* in street."

He nodded. "I'm looking for Anse Jasey."

"*Si.* Señor Jasey 'ave gone." She made a face. "I no like heem."

"How long has he been gone?" Donal put the question in Spanish.

Tulita smiled gratefully, replied in the same tongue. "A few minutes." She paused, a hint of a frown on her smooth brow. "He had changed his clothes. I had to look closer to be sure."

"He fooled me," Donal admitted.

"He does not wear vaquero clothes," the girl said. "It was his purpose to deceive you." She shook her head. "He is a bad man. *Ay Dios mio*! My Pasqual! I fear for him." Tears welled in her eyes.

"Your grandfather came to the Trading Post," Donal said. "He thinks they have Pasqual somewhere close."

"It must be so," declared the girl. "Jasey and those other men were not gone long. Jasey came back to the office and I saw Gober ride away, but not Ferrel."

"I see," Donal said thoughtfully. "You think Ferrel is keeping watch on Pasqual."

"It must be so," she repeated.

He regarded her intently. "You know the other man—Salvador Antista?"

Her eyes clouded. "Pasqual would not tell me much—" She shook her head. "Pasqual was most strange . . . he seemed frightened . . . told me I must not talk about Salvador Antista."

"You mean he was afraid of Antista?"

"No—not that. I do not think he was afraid of Antista. He was afraid for me. I might be in danger if I talked about him." She gestured despairingly. "I am terrified!"

He tried to reassure her. "I trust Pasqual. There

is something we don't understand, but you mustn't worry, Tulita." His warm smile added conviction to his words. "We'll get at the truth, and we'll find Pasqual."

She seemed comforted. "I will pray," she said. "I will pray for him, for you—for all of us." She crossed herself.

"That's right." Donal gave her an admiring look. "You are a brave girl, Tulita." He hesitated. "I will tell you a secret that even Pasqual does not know."

Her dark eyes widened, she stared at him, lips parted breathlessly.

"Pasqual will be the new foreman of Circle C."

Tulita uttered a little squeal, clasped her hands. "Señor! My Pasqual chief of vaqueros!" Her face was radiant. "I will be so proud . . . Pasqual will be so proud—and his mother."

He left her, bubbling with joy, her fears for the moment lost in a rose-colored dawn of wonders to be.

The desk clerk was waiting with obvious relish for his reappearance in the lobby. He said with heavy sarcasm, "Mebbe you won't figger him a liar next time."

Donal halted, looked at him unsmilingly. "You could have told me that was Jasey who passed me on the porch."

The clerk grinned uncertainly. There was an edge to the stranger's voice. He said in an injured tone, "You wasn't givin' me time to tell you nothin', mister. You shot past the desk like a bat out of hell."

Donal eyed him distastefully. "You work for Jasey, don't you?"

The clerk fingered his big mustache uneasily. "Well"—his tone was cautious—"I reckon I do, seein' that he owns this here hotel." He forced a scowl. "Not that it's any of your damn business."

"You'd be surprised," Donal said grimly. "Take my advice and make tracks away from this town before your job blows you into a jail cell." The screen door slammed behind him.

The desk clerk gazed after him. He had the sick look of a man who had taken a solar plexus blow. He got slowly up from his chair and stared around uncertainly with fear-filled eyes as if he wanted to run but did not know where. "Sounded like he meant it," he muttered aloud.

Two cowboys pushed into the lobby, bootheels clattering, spurs rasping. They tipped back dusty hats from hot perspiring faces and exuberantly demanded a room.

"Sure." The desk clerk came out of his daze and gave the register a professional whirl. "You boys in for a little fun, huh?"

"You've guessed it, first shot," chortled one of the men. He scrutinized the man behind the desk, added sympathetically, "You're lookin' some off your feed, feller."

"I ain't feelin' so good," admitted the desk clerk in a wan voice. He paused, brows furrowed in a worried frown. "Did you see that hombre that just went out?"

"Sure did," they chimed.

"Was wonderin' who he was," the clerk said. "Ain't seen him round before."

"You wouldn't," answered one of the men. "Don Cameron's been away more'n a year. Just got back from Cuba, I reckon."

"My gawd," muttered the desk clerk. "Was that *him?*" He drew a handkerchief from his pocket and wiped his suddenly perspiring and ashen face.

Donal was not sure that his warning had been well-timed. The desk clerk might be made of sterner stuff than he seemed. He was inclined to believe otherwise. It was his guess that for all his bluster, the big-bellied man had the heart of a rabbit. If his surmise proved correct, the Daker House was going to lose a desk clerk and Anse Jasey's gang would be minus one more scoundrelly hireling. It was his purpose to use the javelin of fear whenever a chance offered. Bittner's two deputies had already read the writing on the wall and promptly shaken the dust of San Benito from their bootheels. Bittner himself had turned in his sheriff's star and was a captive. Red was headed back to the Cimarron country, and Monte had thrown in his lot with

Circle C. Fargo was lying out in the chaparral under a pile of stones and two more of Gober's renegades lay dead at the Sheep Springs camp. Another man had died up on the ridge trail from Alamo's bullet, and the lone survivor of the Sheep Springs battle was a prisoner at the ranch.

Three men already in flight, a possible fourth. Two prisoners, and four men dead. An amazing tally that filled Donal with mixed emotions, grim satisfaction at the lightning blows that must have rocked Jasey to his heels, a cold certainty that Jasey would strike back, and swiftly. The man would use all the tricks in the box, treachery, bribery, secret murder. It was in the cards that he would fight like a cornered rat.

The mysterious Antista letter worried Donal more than he cared to admit. Antista's assertion that he was a descendant of Don Fidel's brother, Mario, was vouched for by Marica Torres. If he could furnish proof that he was the legal owner of the old Salazar ranch, the grant deed obtained by Donal's father from Don Fidel's sister would be worthless.

The possibilities were appalling. Circle C would be an outfit without a home, without a foot of range. Worse still, Antista could demand heavy damages for more than a quarter of a century's illegal possession. He might lay claim to all the cattle and horses that wore the Circle C iron on their hides. At the best it would mean long and costly litigation.

It was a headache, viewed from any angle; and behind it all lurked the sinister cunning of Jasey's interest in Salvador Antista. The lawyer had been digging in dusty records. He may or may not have unearthed some long-forgotten document that would give color to Antista's claim.

It was a problem that had to be faced, Donal grimly told himself. He racked his brains for the flaw he instinctively sensed lay within his grasp if he only knew where to look. The one weak spot that would blow the Antista business sky high.

A sudden thought narrowed his eyes. The letter! There was something wrong with it, something that had vaguely puzzled him from the start. Antista could not have written that letter. He was presumably an educated Mexican of proud descent. A *caballero.* He would not be guilty of so meanly worded a letter. He would have veiled his threats behind the polite phrasing of his hidalgo breed.

Donal's pulse quickened. It was Jasey who had written the letter. Unfamiliar with the innate courtesy of a well-born Mexican he had made the fatal mistake of using the phraseology of a common border desperado.

The scrambled pieces were falling into their proper places. Jasey had learned of Antista's kinship to the Salazars. If he could establish the Mexican as Don Fidel's rightful heir he would have an unbeatable claim to the ranch. Antista had evidently refused to be a party to the conspiracy, and, alarmed, Jasey had locked him away in some secret hiding place. The fact that the Mexican was apparently still alive indicated that the lawyer regarded him as too valuable a pawn to destroy. He was going to need Antista and hoped to finally break down his resistance. Pasqual Torres had in some way stumbled on the truth and Jasey had taken steps to silence him.

Roderick Dhu listened attentively to his theory. "I'm thinkin' ye're on the right track," he agreed.

"I may be wrong," admitted Donal. "I don't think so." He lit a cigarette and added grimly, "Antista's evidence can put Jasey behind the bars, if nothing else will."

"Ye'll have to find the man first," smiled the trader.

"If old Pedro is right, he's not far away." Donal paused, added thoughtfully, "If Pasqual is still alive we'll find him with Antista."

The trader nodded. "Ay, Jasey would not let him get back to the ranch with the tale Antista could tell him."

"I'm having a talk now with Bittner," Donal decided. "There's a chance he knows where Jasey is keeping Antista."

The two men made their way to the big corral in the rear of the store. Brasca grinned at them from a bench under a hoary cottonwood in front of the barn. “I’ve got Bittner haltered up in a empty stall,” he told Donal with a chuckle. “He ain’t carin’ much for his jail cell, from the way he frets.”

He led the way to the stall where the prisoner lay on a pile of straw. He gave his visitors a venomous look from bloodshot eyes.

“These ropes are too damn tight,” he complained. “Ain’t no sense in tyin’ me up thisaways.”

Donal gave Brasca a nod. “Turn him loose,” he said.

The cowboy reluctantly obeyed. “I’d as soon turn a killin’ wolf loose,” he grumbled. “This here hombre is pizen mean. I ain’t trustin’ him as far as I can throw this barn.”

The ex-sheriff got stiffly to his feet, stood rubbing numbed wrists. “All I ask is a chance to get away from this town,” he said sullenly. “I’m finished.”

“I’ll think it over,” Donal said. The half promise in his voice lifted the prisoner’s head in a quick, hopeful look. Donal continued, “I want a straight answer from you, Bittner. Where have you got Pasqual Torres and Salvador Antista hid out?”

“I wouldn’t know about ’em,” answered the man sulkily. He dropped his eyes under Donal’s steady look. “Seen Torres in the Longhorn,”

Bittner admitted. "He bought me a drink, got to askin' plenty questions about this Antista hombre."

Donal studied the man thoughtfully. He said slowly, "Is that all you can tell me?"

"Sure is," Bittner answered. "I wasn't seein' Torres ag'in after that time in the Longhorn. I figgered he'd headed back to the ranch."

"What makes you think he did?"

"Seen him come out of the post office and fork his saddle," Bittner replied.

"I'll bet the skunk's lyin'," muttered Brasca.

"Is that right, Bittner?" Donal flung the question curtly.

The ex-sheriff's face took on a mottled look. "I ain't lyin'," he denied, sullenly. "I ain't knowin' where Torres went to if it wasn't back to the ranch, and I ain't knowin' a damn thing about the Antista hombre."

"Didn't Jasey tell you anything about him?" persisted Donal.

"Nary a word." Bittner wiped his hot face with the back of his hand.

Donal eyed him discontentedly. The man's story left him dissatisfied. If he were telling the truth, Pasqual had stopped at the post office for the mail and then headed for the ranch. That part of it could easily be true, but it was possible that Pasqual did not get very far from town. He may have been waylaid, shot from ambush and his body concealed in the brush. Or he had been rushed away to some secret hideout. Whatever the answer, Pasqual had not returned to the ranch.

A commotion out in the big corral drew his gaze to the door. Horses, men's voices, the jingle and drag of spurs.

Brasca grinned at him, said placidly, "Sounds like Salty has got in with his Sheep Springs bunch."

Donal was aware of a vast relief. Reinforcements meant he could make an immediate and thorough search for Pasqual Torres.

Salty Wells was looking very pleased with himself. "We sure have been on the jump," he told Donal. "Got them steers over to Cameron and loaded on the cars at sun-up this mornin'."

"That's fine, Salty. What have you done with those Rocking D cows?"

"Got 'em holed up in the Devil's Parlor," grinned the cattle boss. "Plenty of feed there to hold 'em for a spell. Left Omaha and a couple of the boys to keep a lookout."

"I'm mighty glad you boys got here," Donal said. His appraising eyes took in the some half score men watering their horses at the long trough under the cottonwood. He read fatigue in their hot, dusty faces. "You'll want to eat."

"Ain't et since we left Cameron," admitted Salty. His keen eyes regarded Donal intently. "Pasqual ain't showed up, huh?"

Donal shook his head gloomily.

"That's sure bad news." The cattle boss scowled. "Ain't you picked up no sign?"

"Nothing definite." Donal gave him a brief account of his unsuccessful search. "If he's still alive, there's a chance he's somewhere close."

"We'll take this town apart," growled the cattle boss. He slapped his dusty hat violently against brush-scarred leather chaps, added grimly, "We'll sure make plenty bad medicine for the hombres that got him."

13

It seemed to Ruth Merrill that she was in the center of all the loneliness in the world. She sat lightly erect in her saddle, a hint of fear in her eyes as she gazed at the titanic sweep of rugged brown hills. There was a violent look to them that made her think vaguely of mighty cataclysmic forces. The country was so vast, so remote, so menacingly aloof and inhospitable.

She stared with hard, bitter eyes at the savage, bleak hills that rose in folds to dark forested mountain slopes. She would never rest until the men who had murdered her father had paid for their brutal crime. It was not just vengeance she wanted. The thought of such human monsters being allowed to prey on the innocent and unsuspecting revolted her.

She was suddenly aware that the burnished steel of the horizon had taken on a peculiar saffron tinge. The heat waves no longer shimmered on the rocks. Puffs of hot wind came fretfully and she saw little dust devils teetering across the dunes. The stillness was oppressive, only those heated puffs of air searing her face.

She glanced about, conscious of an odd fear constricting her heart. She sensed that the brown horse under her was uneasy. He snorted, sidled about nervously, rebellious of tightened rein. Her own mare was lame after the hard ride from the ranch and Placido had thrown her saddle on Mrs. Cameron's horse. Mrs. Cameron had not entirely approved of the morning ride, and only consented on the promise not to go far from the house. Engrossed with her unhappy memories she must have ridden further than she thought. Perhaps she had been foolish. She recalled Donal Cameron's warning to stay close to the house. The temptation had been too great. A little ride would help her jangled nerves, and it seemed safe enough.

The saffron hue deepened into a brown murk that billowed into the heavens. A rising wind moaned through the chaparral, and flurries of sand rattled like hail against the rocks.

The saw-toothed desert ridges seemed to dissolve in a yellow mist, and the sun became a red, molten disk that suddenly vanished under the blanketing murk.

The meaning of it all came to Ruth with a shock. The horse was wiser than she, had recognized the danger. That brown murk wavering across the sky was sand.

She let the now frantic horse have his head; and then suddenly the wind was shrieking in her ears and the world was snuffed out in an angry brown pall.

The flying sand struck her face, brought tears

streaming from her eyes. She lowered her head to the blast and pulled the frightened horse to a standstill.

Her one thought now was to find some shelter from the stinging onslaught. Blurred shapes whisked past, dead shrubs, weeds, torn from their roots. Something struck the horse's legs and he leaped forward with a frightened snort. She fought with him, again brought him to a standstill. He stood with head down, back humped against the drive of wind and sand. She felt the powerful body under her flinch and tremble. Panic grew in her. She dared not let him have his head and run with the storm. It was impossible to see a thing in that blinding inferno of dust, and the terrain was a death trap of pot-holes and yawning fissures.

The thought of a runaway ride made her giddy with fear. She scrambled from the saddle, stood there, reins clutched in her hand, eyes searching frantically through the murk for some upthrust of rock that would break the fury of flying sand.

She became aware of a new sound, a curious hissing, or whispering. It was her first experience of a desert sandstorm, but instinctively she knew that what she heard was sand, crawling across the desert floor. She was too dangerously close to those shifting dunes. She had heard tales about them, how men and horses had been buried deep in the drifts, and found years later when some new storm uncovered their whitened bones.

She cowered now, under a more ghastly fear. She must move on, put distance between herself and those menacing sand drifts.

She stumbled along blindly, leading the horse. Flying sand stung her smarting eyes, sifted into her hair. She was afraid to breathe for fear of choking, and she began to feel a burning in her tortured lungs.

Boulders rose up in unexpected places and bumped her knees, and twice she stumbled into chuckholes and almost fell headlong. The horse suddenly snorted and jerked back. She pulled on the reins, cried at him desperately. Her attempts to make him budge were useless.

A hint of the truth filtered into her mind as she stood there, helpless, angry. The horse sensed a danger close at hand, something she could not herself see, or had not noticed.

She stared intently in the direction they had been moving, and suddenly the brown murk billowed like a great curtain and she caught a brief glimpse of the yawning chasm an arm's length away.

Chills chased up and down her spine, and very slowly, cautiously, she angled away to the right. This time the horse followed without further protest. She halted and patted him gratefully. She felt she would always love the stubborn brute.

She bumped into a big barrel cactus and recoiled with a cry of pain from its spike-like thorns. It seemed useless to venture in any direction. She would have to wait.

Something was groaning and creaking a few feet away. A tall yucca, she guessed, struggling to hold its own against the press of the wind. She listened fearfully, and suddenly, with a rending crash, the yucca went down.

Ruth glimpsed the great bole driving past them. A tangle of dragging roots side-swiped the horse and with a frenzied snort the animal broke from her grasp and vanished into the blanketing dust.

Sheer fright held her stiffly upright for a moment, and then her legs gave way and she found herself face down on the ground, limp, utterly spent, but conscious of an odd thankfulness. Death had pressed so near to her. A few feet closer and the uprooted yucca would have left her lying there, mangled and lifeless.

She rolled over on her side, but made no attempt to get to her feet. There was nothing she could do. Only wait in patience for the sandstorm to subside. Perhaps the horse would be kind and would wait somewhere near. A vain hope, she decided. It was far more probable that he would make his way back to the ranch. Mrs. Cameron would be dreadfully frightened—and old Alamo. She had not let Alamo know she was going for a ride. He would have objected, or would have insisted on companioning her. She had been foolish, thoughtless, Ruth told herself miserably. She was only getting what she deserved.

Presently she glimpsed the vague bulk of a large boulder. It offered some protection from the stinging sand and she crawled toward it, uttered a little scream as a small animal scurried away from the lee side. A rabbit, she surmised. She had frightened the little creature away from its shelter.

The boulder considerably lessened the force of the storm. She nestled against it with a feeling of gratitude. The storm could not last forever, and the solid rock at her back gave her a feeling of security.

She found a handkerchief and wiped her dust-grimed face. She had lost her hat and her hair was a sand-filled tangle. Her flannel shirt had pulled loose from the belt. She tucked it back, discovered numerous torn places. She was going to look like something the cat dragged in, she reflected ruefully. Her cowboy pants seemed intact. They were tough and durable, the copper-riveted blue overalls all cowboys swore by.

She became aware of a curious sensation in her ears and realized with some amazement that the wind had stopped its fiendish screaming. The sudden stillness seemed unreal. Unutterable relief flowed through her. The sandstorm was over.

She continued to wait. The air was still heavy

with dust, and visibility practically nil. It was senseless to move from her sheltering boulder until she could see where she was going.

Gradually the sun appeared. It looked like a great red orange, and then slowly the harsh landscape swam into view through a pale yellow sea of light.

Ruth got to her feet and searched her surroundings with eager eyes for some sign of the horse. Her heart sank. It had been a vain hope. She was faced with the unpleasant prospect of finding her way back to the ranch on foot. Of course, the appearance of the riderless horse would raise the alarm and men would be searching for her. The thought failed to cheer her. They would not know where to search. The country was so vast, and interlaced with canyons that looked so disconcertingly alike. It might be hours, days, before the searchers found her.

She gazed about despondently, and with fast-growing alarm. She could not be certain from which direction she had come. She could recognize nothing to guide her, no helpful landmark. Only rocks and shrubs and barren slopes, the myriad ravines and canyons. She was completely lost. One direction offered as much hope as another.

She trudged along, uncomfortably aware now that the sun had resumed its normal brassy glare. It was unbearably hot, and the shimmering heat waves on the rocks made her dizzy. She longed for a drink of water.

She paused in the scant shade of a gaunt greasewood bush and gazed about her despairingly, and for some reason or other found herself thinking of Donal Cameron. She had the feeling that he was standing with his back to a huge split boulder, watching her with unsmiling, disapproving eyes. She could see him so distinctly, tall and lean, the heavy gun in the holster tied down to his thigh, the almost haughty cast of his face, his resolute, steady eyes. They were not unsmiling now, but compassionate, warm, full of grave concern, and something else that quickened the beat of her heart, made her call his name softly. She said, "Donal, *Donal!*"

The sound of her own voice caused her to jump. She was unconscious of having spoken aloud. She laughed hysterically, and again the sound made her start. She was imagining such nonsense. She must be going crazy.

She said aloud, angrily, "I've got to stop it! I've got to think this thing out coolly, the way he would, the way Alamo would."

Something stirred under the branches of the greasewood. Ruth looked down, held her breath as she saw a flat, venomous head, the thick, mottled coils. The warning whirr of the rattles sounded again, and with a horrified exclamation she sprang aside and hurried away. The rattlesnake could have the shade to himself, she decided with a shudder.

The incident aroused a new fear in her, the danger of failing to see one of the crawling things in time. She must be on the watch for them. She halted every few feet and scrutinized the ground, the withdrawn shade of the bushes. The position of the sun told her it was midday and she had heard that rattlesnakes invariably sought out shady spots during the heated hours. Alamo had told her that snakes disliked the direct glare of the noonday sun. Especially sidewinders. They would die in a few hours.

She stumbled along cautiously, eyes wary, ears alert. There was one comforting thing about a rattlesnake. It did give warning of its intentions. Rattlesnakes were not deliberate, vicious killers like Al Gober and his kind.

A low ridge had been beckoning her. It was possible that by climbing to its highest point she could locate her position, perhaps discover some landmark that would suggest the trail from which she had wandered. She racked her memory for some ridge that would seem familiar if she saw it. She had not been very observant, she decided unhappily. She couldn't recall a thing.

She toiled up the steep slope, conscious of a growing panic. She would never find her way back to the ranch. She was going to wander around, hopelessly lost, until she died of thirst and exhaustion. Someday they would find her, but the buzzards would have been there first. Only sun-bleached bones would mark the spot where she had died.

She fought desperately to put the morbid thoughts from her. She must hang on to her courage, keep her mind clear and refuse to let panic ride her. Anything less than the best in her would indeed prove her undoing.

She finally reached the top of the ridge, breathless, her legs wobbly, her heart pounding, and found herself standing on an overhanging ledge. The slope on this side dropped precipitously into a wide canyon, a descent of some hundred yards. She saw a tangle of stunted piñon trees, and close-growing brush, but best of all, she saw a thin spiral of pale blue smoke. A campfire, or perhaps a squatter's cabin.

Ruth edged further along the ledge, trying for a better look. A cabin would mean water down there, a spring, for she could see no sign of a flowing stream. It *was* a cabin! She could faintly see the stovepipe elbowing through the split-log wall.

Sudden doubts assailed her, held her irresolute. The wisp of smoke was proof that the cabin was occupied. Perhaps a line rider, or some kindly woman, helping her man make a home in this remote wilderness. Or it was possible that danger lay down there. The place might be some desperado's hideout.

The sun was burning her to a crisp. The heated rocks were like live coals under her feet. She had to do something before she collapsed. Her head felt queer and the landscape seemed to waver drunkenly before her eyes. She *must* find water, and there *was* water—where that smoke beckoned.

She started down, stumbling, sliding, crawling over boulders that gave no footing at all. Cat's-claw dug cruel barbed hooks into her flesh, tore more holes in her flannel shirt. She pushed on in a frenzy of desperation. *She had to reach that water, or she would die.* The thought spurred her on. She forgot about deadly rattlesnakes, took no heed of clawing thorns, the bleeding scratches on her arms and face.

Somehow she reached the floor of the canyon, and staggered slowly toward the wisp of smoke curling above the trees. She saw a pole corral, and horses, and suddenly a man, standing in the doorway of the cabin. She beckoned to him feebly, tried to speak, and then her legs gave way and she felt herself falling.

Faintly, as from a long distance, she heard voices, dimly saw a man's face bending close to hers, a round moon face covered with a stubble of beard. A vaguely familiar face, with its cold staring eyes and the thin slit of a mouth so like a shark's. She heard him say, "It's the Merrill girl, Squint. Go git some water, feller—"

Horror constricted Ruth's heart. She gave a low, terrified moan, beat at the grinning face with impotent fists, and fainted.

14

The faint haze of dust lifting on the mesa beyond Tule Creek drew speculative comments from the two men leaning over the corral gate.

"She don't move natcheral, that dust drift," observed Alamo Jones. "You watch her close, Bearcat."

"Sure don't," agreed Bearcat. His eyes took on a worried squint. "Moves 'round kind of crazy, like one of them dust devils. Kind of teeters this way and that, and then fades away."

"Looks like the bronc ain't got no rider," Alamo said. "Stops to grab him a bit of bunch grass, and that's when you don't see dust. Then he gits to runnin' like he was in a hurry, sees a good-lookin' bunch of grass off to one side and heads that way."

"Which same makes him some erratical," Bearcat said.

"Waal," Alamo's tone was doubtful, "you cain't prove that thar word, by me, Bearcat. I was brung up to talk plain American lingo." He continued to stare at the dust haze. "Ain't likin' it," he went on worriedly. "She orter been back a hour ago."

The two men exchanged long looks, and each read in the other's eyes the same gnawing anxiety they could no longer conceal.

"I'll fork a saddle and take a look at that bronc," Alamo said.

"A smart idee," agreed Bearcat. He gnawed off a chew of plug tobacco, gaze following the gaunt old mountain man as he moved with his long bent-kneed stride across the yard to the barn. "Kin sure git over the ground fast," he muttered admiringly.

A voice hailed him from the garden gate and he saw Mrs. Cameron beckoning him.

"I'm dreadfully worried," she began as he approached. "I'm afraid something has happened." Her tone was self-reproachful, disturbed. "I shouldn't have let her go, but she was so restless, and she promised not to go far."

"I wouldn't git to feelin' scary, ma'am," counseled the Circle C man. "You know how it is with a gal. Kind of gits to thinkin' and ridin' along and not noticin' whar she is and how long she's been gone."

Mrs. Cameron looked at him sharply. She sensed lack of conviction in his voice. "You're upset, yourself," she charged.

His eyes lowered guiltily. "Waal, ma'am, I ain't callin' you a liar. Me and Alamo figgers there's mebbe somethin' gone wrong with her."

Her look fastened on Alamo, spurring his horse into a run across the yard. "Where is he going?" she asked. The fear deepened in her eyes.

"Now don't you git to frettin', ma'am," Bearcat

said with a gruffness he was far from feeling. He had a deep fondness for Mrs. Cameron and could not bear to see her worried.

She repressed an annoyed rejoinder. His intentions were well meant. "You're as bad as Brasca," she said, smiling at him. "You two old-timers should know by now that I don't tremble at the sight of trouble." There was a break in her voice that made Bearcat wince. "I learned from my husband how to meet trouble."

"You sure got Circle C blood in you," Bearcat said gently. "Ain't no time when Circle C ever turned tail on trouble. Warn't old Don's way to back up from nobody no time."

"I wish he were here," Mrs. Cameron said in a low voice. "We've got to do the best we can, Bearcat, and carry on. That is what you said the other night, that Circle C would carry on."

"We sure will, ma'am," Bearcat said earnestly. "I'm backin' the boy to fill his hand with plenty aces." He paused, and an awed look crept into his eyes. "Gits me to feelin' queer when I look at him, hear his voice, see the way he sets a saddle. He's the spittin' image of his dad twenty years back."

Mrs. Cameron's grateful smile lingered on him, and then, briskly, "I want to know where Alamo has gone."

Bearcat told her about the riderless horse on the mesa. "Alamo figgered to have a look," he said. "There's a chance she got throwed."

"I've ridden Brownie for years," Mrs. Cameron pointed out. "That horse is as gentle as a lamb. He wouldn't buck the girl off."

"Waal"—Bearcat politely turned his head and spat out a dark brown stream of tobacco juice—"I warn't sayin' the old hoss mebbe done some pitchin'. Lot of things could happen, like steppin' in a hole, or gettin' skeered at a rattler."

"We'll hope it's nothing worse," Mrs. Cameron said. She was staring intently at the wagon road that snaked through the chaparral toward San Benito. "I wonder if that is Donal coming?" Excitement put color in her cheeks.

Bearcat studied the dust drift appraisingly. "If it's him, he's got a bunch of the boys trailin' along, from the looks of the dirt they're kickin' up," he commented.

"I can't wait to know," exclaimed Mrs. Cameron. "I'll get the glasses." She ran back to the house, skirts flying.

Bearcat continued to watch the approaching cloud of dust. He was lean, and sun-dried, and for all his years, as tough and durable as well-cured rawhide. His chill, slow-measuring eyes gave him a grim, formidable look, but his friends knew that under the harsh exterior was an odd gentleness, a stanch loyalty.

His shaggy brows drew down in a worried frown as he noted the rapid approach of the billowing dust. Whoever the riders were, they were coming fast.

He threw an impatient glance back at the house. He was anxious to get the glasses on that bunch of hard-riding horsemen. These were times when anything could happen. If those riders were on an unfriendly mission, it meant gunsmoke and plenty of it.

He held out a hand for the glasses as Mrs. Cameron ran into the yard, followed by Marica Torres. She hesitated, then surrendered the binoculars. His grim expression sent a foreboding chill through her.

The two women stood there, silent, hardly daring to breathe, eyes intent on him as he studied the approaching riders through the powerful glasses. They saw the grim lines of his face suddenly relax. Mrs. Cameron let out a sigh of relief.

Bearcat lowered the glasses and gave her a grin. "Yeah," he said. "It's him, and Brasca, and some of the boys from Sheep Springs." He had the glasses at his eyes again. "Can make out Salty Wells . . . yeah, and I reckon that's Scarface sidin' Shorty and Chico."

Marica gave him a piteous look. "You no see my Pasqual?" Her voice was shrill with anxiety.

Bearcat shook his head, and then said, awkwardly, "Plenty dust flyin'. Cain't see awful good." A kindly, well-intentioned lie. He had scrutinized each one of those horsemen, hoping to recognize Pasqual among them.

Marica was not deceived. With an agonized look at Mrs. Cameron she turned abruptly and fled into the patio.

Hoofs drummed up the avenue, and Alamo tore into the yard. He had the brown horse on a lead-rope. He swung down from his saddle and tossed the rope to Bearcat. "Git her saddle on a fresh horse," he said. "I'm startin' out now to hunt sign for her."

Bearcat hurried toward the barn with the horse following at a slow trot at the end of the rope. His bawling voice brought Placido to the stable door, pitchfork in hand.

"Git this saddle throwed on the bay mare quick," Bearcat told him.

The Mexican vanished inside the barn, and giving the brown horse a slap that sent him following on Placido's heels, Bearcat broke into a run toward the horse corral.

"Looks like the gal got lost in that sandstorm," Alamo said to Mrs. Cameron. "That brown horse shows plenty sign."

Mrs. Cameron nodded. Her experienced eyes had told her the story. "I'm dreadfully frightened," she said. "She—she'd be so helpless."

"I'll need a canteen of water," Alamo said. "Mebbe some whiskey—and things."

By the time Placido had Ruth's saddle changed to the bay mare, Mrs. Cameron had gathered the necessary articles, including a medicine kit. Alamo tied the bag to his saddle and swung up to his horse.

"Don and the boys are coming," Mrs. Cameron told him. She gestured at the distant haze of dust. "They'll be here in a few minutes." She forced herself to speak hopefully. "We'll find her, Alamo."

"I ain't waitin'," Alamo said. His dejected tone told of gaunt fears stalking him. "I'm mighty skeered that she's needin' help bad."

She watched him go, conscious of the same dreadful thought. It was no ordinary range accident that had sent the horse home without its rider.

Bearcat's bawling voice had summoned others to the horse corral. Mrs. Cameron saw Dave Herne, and the new man, Monte, streaking from the bunkhouse. Epifanio already had his rope on a snorting pinto and was leading the animal from the corral.

They went about it with amazing efficiency. Armed with six-guns and rifles, canteen and supplies strapped to their saddles, the searching party vanished down the avenue in a cloud of dust.

Mrs. Cameron impatiently watched the bigger dust drift now less than a mile distant. Marica stood by her side, wringing her hands and muttering prayers to her special saint. "*Ay Dio mio*! My Pasqual! And now the poor señorita. The curse of the Salazars ees weeth thees rancho."

Mrs. Cameron took no notice of her. She was watching the tell-tale dust that hazed above the avenue trees. The roar of pounding hoofs filled her ears, and suddenly the outfit was pouring into the yard.

Donal checked his horse as she ran toward him. The look in her eyes told him that something was wrong. He slid from his saddle, and the horse moved on to join the others at the water trough under the shady trees.

"Don—" She was finding it hard to tell him. "It—it's Ruth . . . We don't know where she is."

He said quietly, "You mean she's lost?"

"She went riding this morning—alone. Her horse came back without her." Mrs. Cameron looked at him compassionately. She had divined his feelings for the girl from Rocking D. She added gently, "We'll find her."

"Yes," he said huskily. "We've got to find her. We *will* find her."

"Alamo is out looking now," Mrs. Cameron continued. "All of them, except Flapjack. He couldn't go because of that rustler he brought in from Sheep Springs. He was wild to go, but Bearcat said it wouldn't be safe to leave the *carcel* unguarded."

Donal's look went reflectively to the men and horses grouped at the long trough under the trees. "We'll get our saddles on fresh horses and start out," he told his mother.

She was grateful for his self-control. "You are so like your father, Don." Her voice choked. "I know how dreadfully you feel, but you don't falter, lose your head." She was suddenly brisk. "I'll tell Rafaela to put up sandwiches. They'll be ready by the time you've changed horses." She paused, gave him a bright glance. "Stormy is in the stable."

Salty Wells looked at him sharply as he approached the trough. "Bad news, huh?"

Donal told him briefly about the missing girl. "We've got to find her, Salty." The pain in his hard, tight voice made the cattle boss wince.

"Sure we'll find her," he said gruffly.

"Have the boys throw their saddles on fresh horses," Donal told him. "We'll stick Bittner in the *carcel* with the man we picked up at Sheep Springs." He paused. "Nobody on the place but Flapjack. Pick out a couple of the boys to stand watch on the *carcel* with him."

Salty said he would attend to the matter, and Donal overtook Brasca on his way to the barn with his jaded horse. The old cowboy was frankly pessimistic.

"Might mean anythin'," he said gloomily. "Might mean that Gober's gang got hold of her.

They'd figger it would be a smart trick to turn her horse loose, git us to thinkin' she's been throwed and mebbe killed. The skunks would know we could comb the range till hell froze and never find her . . . never be sure she warn't layin' dead some place."

"Where would they take her, Brasca?" Donal's face had a gray look.

"It's my guess they'd head back to Rockin' D with her."

"It's a hunch," Donal muttered.

Brasca peeled off his saddle and turned to lift it to its peg. He halted the motion and stared intently at the younger man.

"Yeah?" His tone was gently questioning.

"That's right," Donal said. "I'm having a look over there."

"I'll git me a fresh bronc," Brasca said. He turned to the stable door, saddle gear slung over a shoulder.

"You're not going," Donal said firmly.

"Figger to go alone, huh?"

"That's right," Donal said again.

"You doggone fool," fumed Brasca.

"It's a one-man job," Donal pointed out. "You're not going anywhere, Brasca. I want you to stick close to the house. We can't leave the women unprotected."

Brasca wrathfully slammed his saddle on the peg. "You're the boss, son."

"Flapjack will have his hands full, playing jailer," Donal continued. "I'm leaving a couple of the boys to stand guard with him. That old 'dobe isn't so good any more."

"Thar's chinks in them mud walls you can stick your hand through," asserted Brasca. "A smart hombre like Bittner could easy bust out."

"That's why I'm leaving a couple of the boys with Flapjack," Donal reminded curtly. "Get my saddle for me. It's out there on the horse I rode in from town."

"Sure." Brasca hurried into the yard, and Donal reached Stormy's bridle from its peg and went into the stall. The black horse greeted him with a low nicker. He seemed in good shape, eager for a run.

Brasca reappeared with the saddle, and stood watching while Donal got the horse ready.

"Salty has fixed for Chico and Shorty to stay with Flapjack," he said. "He figgered to leave Scarface, 'stead of Chico, but I told him he'd be a fool not to take Scarface along. Scarface has got a Injun nose for followin' a trail. That hombre can read sign in the dark of the moon." Brasca nodded solemnly. "He's most as good as me and Bearcat."

"You two old range hawks," grinned Donal. He drew his rifle from the saddle-boot, examined it carefully.

Brasca grinned back at him. The bond between

them was strong. "You don't need to worry about your ma, son," he said softly. "I'll stick so close she'll figger I'm a burr the wind's blowed into the yard."

Mrs. Cameron was waiting near the patio gate with a packet of sandwiches and a fresh canteen of water. He told her briefly of Brasca's hunch about Ruth.

"You're going there—alone?" Her tone was grave, but held no hint of protest.

He nodded, finished tying the canteen to the saddle and slipped the packet of sandwiches in his pocket.

"Pray God you'll be in time, son," she said, and she kissed him gently, added in a low voice, "I know how much she means to you."

He could not trust himself to speak. There was a choke in his throat. He turned from her quickly and was suddenly in the saddle and riding away.

Mrs. Cameron watched him go, the fear she would not let him see now in her eyes. She stood there until the dust kicked up by the black horse dwindled to a faint golden haze in the distance.

15

Ruth could hear the low murmur of men's voices from somewhere behind her. She made no effort to lift her head and look. For the moment she was content to lie there under the shading branches of the tree.

A wind fluttered the green leaves, gave her glimpses of blue sky. The stillness was complete—and restful. The dream, though, was spoiled by those nightmarish voices. She would wake up, hear herself screaming.

Ruth opened her eyes again, and this time she knew that she was not dreaming. It was all too dreadfully real. She sat up, and the movement sent little trickles of water down her face. She touched her hair. It was sopping wet, and when her fingertips explored her face they came away grimed with mud.

She was remembering everything, now, and the reality was far worse than the dream. She wanted to turn her head and look at the men behind her. Sheer terror held her motionless. She could only stare, wide-eyed, at the pole corral beyond the tree. There were horses, drowsing in the sun, and a flop-eared burro, nosing at the water in a wooden trough. She counted the horses mechanically. Four of them, and on the nearest animal she could distinctly make out the brand. Her own Rocking D. It was too absurd. She wanted to laugh, but to laugh now would mean hysteria, and she must keep her sanity, draw deep on her courage, sharpen her wits.

Something dangled from a tree beyond the corral. The branch from which it hung swayed gently in the wind, and the *thing* swayed with it, literally danced on air.

Horror filled the girl's eyes. It was a man, hanging there from the tree. *A dead man.*

She sprang to her feet and started to run. She must get away. It was too dreadful . . . more than she could bear. A hand fastened on her arm, held her powerless to move.

"Take it easy, Miss Merrill—"

She choked down the beginnings of a scream. She had to hold on to herself, or she would be lost, completely at the mercy of these men.

She looked at the man confronting her, aware now of an odd calmness in her. She was frightened, terribly so, but her nerves were again under control.

She said quietly, "Let go of me." Her eyes blazed at him. "How dare you?"

"Now, ma'am—" Ferrel's shark mouth split in a wide grin that made Ruth repress a shudder. "You ain't yourself right now—"

"Let go of me," she repeated.

His hand dropped from her arm. "You had a

close call," he said. "We thought you was a goner when you come staggerin' down the slope. Went off in a dead faint. We done all we could. Doused you with water and got you under the tree, out of the sun." He nodded solemnly. "You was in mighty bad shape."

His respectful, almost apologetic manner, mystified her, also increased her growing self-assurance. It was apparent that Ferrel was disposed to be friendly.

Ruth turned and looked at Squint who had not stirred from the log against which he indolently sprawled. The leer on his ugly dark face was like a blow. Her heart sank. There was no friendliness in that evil smirk. Only wicked laughter at some hideous jest at her expense.

She willed herself to speak quietly, naturally. "Finding water here was a miracle. I'm ever so grateful for your help."

"I'm mighty glad you run into our camp here, ma'am."

Ruth was sure now that the words were a covert sneer. She wanted to scream at him, tell him she knew that he was a murderer, that they were both murderers. She smiled instead, or tried to smile. She knew the result must have been a rather ghastly grimace under the smear of yellow dust that masked her face.

She said with an attempt at lightness, "Well, I'm well out of the woods, now, or the sandstorm, thanks to you and Squint." Her look went to the corral. "If you will lend me a horse, I'll find my way home."

She felt their calculating grins on her, sensed rather than saw their swift exchange of amused looks.

Ferrel said slowly, "Well, now, Miss Merrill, you ain't in no shape yet to go wanderin' off ag'in." He shook his head regretfully. "At that, we ain't got a spare horse we could loan you right now."

She made a show of indignation. "After all, I'm your boss, Ferrel—" She gestured at the corral. "Those are certainly Rocking D horses—*my* horses."

The other man laughed raucously, and Ferrel said harshly, "Shut your face, Squint. Where's your manners?"

"He's drunk," Ruth said contemptuously, and stared pointedly at the bottle that stood on the stump.

Ferrel ignored the comment. He motioned toward the cabin. "You come inside and wash up, Miss Merrill. Squint and me was fixin' to eat when you showed up. He'll slap on some extry bacon for you. You'll feel better for some food and hot coffee."

"I don't want to go inside!" Despite her resolutions, there was panic in her voice. "I want to go home—*now.*"

"I reckon not, ma'am." Ferrel's voice was suddenly hard. "I'm knowin' best, and I'm wantin' you inside. When Squint and me get done with our bus'ness here, we'll take you along with us."

She loosened the reins. "How dare you talk to me so impudently?" she flared. "I'm the boss of Rocking D. I give the orders . . . not you."

He was conciliatory again. "Now, ma'am . . . you ain't yourself—yet—" He met Squint's look and tapped his head significantly. "That sandstorm, and losin' her horse has upset her mind, I reckon."

"Is sure actin' loco," grinned the half-breed. "Want for me to git a rope on her?"

"Ain't wantin' to tie her up—not yet," Ferrel said reflectively. "I reckon she ain't *that* bad, Squint. Only kind of loose in her mind. We'll have to sort of gentle her down, git her back to the ranch so Anse Jasey can look after her."

Ruth understood their game now. They were pretending she had lost her mind, planned to take her back to Rocking D—to Jasey. The thought made her ill.

She said desperately, "I'm not going back to Rocking D . . . I won't!"

"Mr. Jasey will be mighty glad to see you back safe, ma'am." Ferrel's grin was diabolical. "He's been mighty worried, you runnin' off the way you done. He figgered you was sick in your mind, on account of your pa gettin' drowned in the crik."

The man's hand was on her arm again, gently, but firmly, as if he would soothe distraught nerves. "You come along with me, ma'am. I'll take right good care of you, git you back to the ranch safe."

Ruth flinched under the touch, but made no attempt to resist. She saw clearly that to use her puny strength against these men would only make matters worse. She was helpless, completely in their power.

The cabin wore the dejected look of long years of neglect. It was possible the place had once been the beginnings of some squatter's dream. Whatever the reason for its being, it was no longer the abode of honest men. There were cracks in the split-log walls where the mud that once chinked them had crumbled to dust. Holes gaped in the roof and the accumulated debris of years littered the mud floor.

It was plain even to Ruth that this was a place long since abandoned to the wilderness, and that it was now nothing more than a hideout for men like Ferrel and his fellow desperado.

Her legs felt like rubber under her. Despite her reluctance she was obliged to sit down on a rickety rawhide chair that received her weight with a protesting creak.

A tangle of brush and creeping vines covered the two small windows from which the glass had long disappeared, and the result was a depressing and sinister gloom that added to her despair.

The half-breed was slicing bacon into a pan. She watched him dully. He used a long knife that he drew from under his shirt. He was the kind of man who would carry a concealed knife. It was very sharp. It sliced through the bacon like butter. He wiped the blade on his greasy pants, pushed it back in its hidden sheath and reached for the battered tin coffee pot.

Ferrel came in with a rusty pan he had filled with spring water. He placed it on the dilapidated table, and after a brief hesitation she got up and rinsed her hands. Her eyes felt caked with dust and she used the wet handkerchief on them, but made no attempt to wash her face or do anything to her tangled hair. She was conscious of Ferrel's eyes, of the half-breed's furtive glances as he worked at the little cookstove. Their ill-concealed interest enraged her, made her uneasy. She returned as quickly as she could to the rawhide chair. She felt utterly miserable—and frightened.

The half-breed brought her bacon and sliced bread on a tin plate, and coffee in a tin cup. She was inclined to refuse, but wisely decided to eat while she had the chance. Food meant strength, and she was going to need all the strength she could muster if she was to escape from the trap into which she had blundered.

The two men went outside with their bacon sandwiches and tin cups of coffee. Ruth could not see them, but she could hear the low monotone of their voices, and presently the crunch of their boots as they moved on around the side of the cabin. She resisted a wild impulse to dash out through the door. It would be useless. They would be on her before she had gone ten yards. Also her .32 revolver had vanished from its holster. They must have removed it during her brief faint. She had not discovered the loss until a few moments ago when feeling in her pockets for another handkerchief.

She was curious to find out what they were doing on the other side of the cabin. She got stealthily out of the chair, put the plate and cup on the table and tip-toed to the window.

It was impossible to see through the dense tangle of shrubbery that blocked the window and she was about to give up the idea when she noticed the sunlit crack between the logs where the mud had crumbled away. She put her eyes to the opening, drew her head back with a stifled gasp.

Her senses reeled. The man lying out there was bound hand and foot, and the half-breed was bending over him with his long knife.

Ruth forced herself to look again. Her first fears subsided. Squint was not going to kill the helpless prisoner. He was cutting the tightly-knotted rope that bound his ankles.

She continued to watch while the man got

slowly to his feet. He was tall and pantherish, and the dark eyes in his swarthy face burned with rage and contempt. Ruth guessed he was a Mexican. She was also aware of something more she knew about him. This man must be the missing Pasqual Torres.

She remembered the lifeless body hanging from the tree, and a new fear turned like a knife in her heart. She leaned against the dust-grimed wall, sick with dreadful apprehension. They were going to hang him, as they had hung the other man. This was the business Ferrel had said he must finish before they took her back to the ranch. They were going to leave Pasqual Torres dangling at the end of a rope.

The thought revolted her. She had to stop them . . . she must stop them. She was not going to let them murder Donal Cameron's friend.

She fled through the door into the hot sunlight and on around the cabin. Ferrel muttered an astonished oath and jerked his gun from holster.

Ruth halted, eyes blazing in her pale face. She said fiercely, "No! You mustn't!"

She heard a muttered exclamation from the Mexican. "*Por Dios*!" Amazement, hope, flashed in his eyes. And then Ferrel's iron grip was on her wrist.

"You keep out of this!" Fury distorted his face.

Ruth wrenched free from his grasp, faced him defiantly, hands clenched. "I won't keep out of it!" Her voice was breathless but unafraid. "I won't let you hang him."

"Huh?" Ferrel glared. "We ain't stringin' him up."

"I saw the other man," she said fiercely. "Hanging from that tree. You murdered him—"

Ferrel had control of himself again. "You're loco." He grinned round at the half-breed who had his long knife pressed against the Mexican's breast. "She sure gits queer notions, huh, Squint?"

"I said we had orter tie her up," growled the half-breed. "The gal's crazy."

The widening grin on Ferrel's face did not touch his bulging marble eyes. Ruth shrank from the cold malignance in them.

He said softly, "We ain't likin' your talk. I reckon we'll tie you up . . . mebbe tie your mouth, too."

"No!" Her hands lifted in protest.

His look went speculatively to the thin cord the half-breed had cut from the Mexican's ankles. "I've a notion to," he said slowly. "Can't have you tellin' lies about us hangin' fellers from trees."

"I'm not lying," she said, faintly.

"You've got what they call haloocinations." Ferrel shook his head. "You ain't seen no dead man swingin' at the end of a rope. Savvy?" He picked up the thin cord.

The tall Mexican broke his silence. "Do not argue with them, señorita. It will do you no good."

"They are going to hang you, too." Her voice broke. "I can't bear it."

"No, señorita. They will not hang me."

"That's right," Ferrel said, nodding his head. "We ain't hangin' you . . . not right now."

The look on his face gave her the creeps. She gazed helplessly at the Mexican. He was a brave man, this Pasqual Torres. She would have liked to call him by name, tell him that Donal Cameron was doing his best to find him. Instinct warned her to be cautious. It might only add to his peril to let these men realize that she knew the prisoner's identity. If chance came she could give Pasqual Torres some small hope. For the present she must guard her secret knowledge.

There was a hint of a smile in his courageous eyes, an unspoken message of hope for herself. She gave him the glimmer of an answering smile and turned away.

Ferrel showed an odd relief. "Wasn't wantin' to tie you up," he said. His eyes shifted in a look at the half-breed. "All right. You git started with him. I'll follow with Miss Merrill."

Ruth, glancing back as he spoke, saw a flicker of excitement in the Mexican's eyes. She knew he had recognized her name, would know who she was. She found cheer in the thought.

She waited in a fever of impatience near the cabin door. She had no wish to go inside. The place smelled of dark deeds and she wanted no more of it.

Ferrel joined her in a few minutes. She saw with relief that he was not disposed to any familiarities now they were left alone. She had rather dreaded being alone with him. It was probably fear of Anson Jasey that held him in leash. He regarded her as Jasey's woman, and anything that was Jasey's meant hands off. The future offered untold terrors, but for the moment she was in no danger from this brutal ruffian.

He said, curtly, "Soon as I git the saddles throwed on we'll git started for the ranch. You stay over there under that tree where I can keep an eye on you from the corral."

Ruth nodded, moved to the tree. She was glad that she could not see the dead man from where she stood.

Ferrel's gaze followed her. "Don't git notions," he warned. "Ain't wantin' trouble from you."

"I won't run away," she said, her eyes disdainful. "I wouldn't get very far."

"I wouldn't want to kill you," grinned the man. "You're too purty."

He stood there, staring at her, an ugly, avid gleam in his eyes that drove the blood from her face. He saw the quick terror mount in her and seemed amused.

"No call to git skeered," he chortled. "Was just thinkin' that Anse Jasey is sure goin' to be mighty glad to see you."

Relief flowed through her as he moved away toward the pole corral, a relief that as quickly faded into the dark horizon of fear inspired by his words.

She closed her eyes, fought resolutely against rising panic. Something would happen . . . something *must* happen. It was a wordless prayer, and again she had the odd feeling that Donal Cameron was close to her, that he was watching her, encouraging her. She could see his face, his steady, resolute eyes.

It was Ferrel's harsh voice that snatched her back to realities. He was approaching, leading the horses.

"All set," he said. "Shortened the stirrups so you can set in the saddle more easy. The feller that used this saddle had legs some longer than yourn." His tone was callous. "He ain't got no use for it no more."

Ruth repressed a shudder and climbed mutely on to the horse. She knew what he meant. He spoke the dreadful truth. The lifeless man swinging from the tree would indeed have no more need for the saddle under her.

16

Some three miles out from the ranch, Donal left the mesa road and pointed the black horse toward the high red cliffs of Rubio Canyon. He was remembering that in the higher reaches of that gloomy gorge was an old Indian trail, now seldom used and, in fact, little known except by a few old-timers. Long before the coming of the white man, Apache warriors had followed its devious twistings through the rugged hills. Its importance to Donal at this moment was the knowledge that the trail eventually dropped into the west fork of Aliso Creek Canyon, less than a mile below the old Daker ranch house.

It was unlikely that Gober had heard of the old Apache war trail. He was a newcomer in the Rio Seco country. His vigilance would be concentrated on the known trails from Circle C—the San Benito road. He would not be on guard against a back-door approach.

He rode slowly, eyes alert for landmarks. Numerous cloudbursts had obliterated many of them. The trunks of uprooted trees, and huge boulders, littered the canyon floor. The treacherous footing made it slow work for the horse.

The high cliffs closed in, drew the sky to a thin

blue line and seemed to shut out all sound of life except the scrape of shod hoofs, the clatter of stones, the creak of saddle leather.

The gloom wrapped around Donal like a dark blanket, bred in him growing doubts and fears. His search in San Benito had failed to uncover any trace of the missing Pasqual Torres. He was beginning to lose hope. Pasqual was dead, a victim of Jasey's diabolical cunning.

He had underestimated Jasey, Donal reflected bitterly. It was not going to be easy to tear from him the robe of respectability he wore, unmask the wolf beneath the lawyer's coat. His genial exterior and smooth talk had lulled suspicion, bred liking and trust in a surprising number of ranchers and townsmen. Jasey's popularity was an appalling fact. He was lavish with his money, and Donal recalled with a wry glance that even his mother had acknowledged the man's charm.

There were those who had openly resented Donal's blunt inferences that Jasey was responsible for the mysterious disappearance of Pasqual Torres. And they had indignantly denied having any knowledge of a Mexican known as Salvador Antista. It was a denial that profoundly perplexed Donal. He had found no one who would admit to Antista's presence in San Benito, or to ever having heard the name.

If it had not been for Marica Torres and pretty Tulita Anda, he would have been inclined to regard the Antista letter as an absurd attempt by Jasey to build up a fictitious claimant. But Marica had declared there was such a man, and Tulita had admitted that Pasqual Torres had spoken of him to her. He had also warned the girl it would be dangerous for her to divulge that he knew Antista.

Apparently, the same knowledge was equally dangerous to others, so dangerous that steps had been taken to bury Pasqual's secret with him in an unknown grave.

The affair was a scrambled puzzle that Donal was unable to put together. He could not find any pieces that made sense. Even Roderick Dhu was baffled and inclined to agree with Brasca that Pasqual might after all be the murderer of Rusty Cross and had fled the country. One fact alone had resulted from the exhaustive search for the Mexican—the discouraging truth that Anson Jasey was strongly entrenched in San Benito. The fact that he had been able to elect his own man as sheriff proved his power.

There were those who regarded Bittner's election as fraudulent and were talking of an investigation—such men as Clover of the Bar 7, Roderick Dhu, Billy Winch and Sam Luther, all of them old-timers who bitterly resented Jasey's growing power and suspected his secret tie-up with the lawless elements infiltrating the town.

Donal was not at all confident that he had heard

the last of the Bittner affair. A lot of people in San Benito regarded Bittner as the legally-elected sheriff. Donal had resisted him, given him a beating and taken his gun and badge of office. He had also brought the sheriff in his own handcuffs to the ranch and thrown him in the ranch *carcel.* It was true that Bittner had confessed that the attempted arrest was a frame-up engineered by Jasey, and that no warrant had been sworn out. Bittner had expected trouble and planned to kill his prisoner. He would have claimed self-defense in the performance of his duty and been cleared of blame.

The affair had been touch and go. Donal's swift action had spoiled the plan to eliminate him, and the sheriff was out of the picture for the moment. There was a chance his friends would demand his release. Donal was grimly determined to get him into a jail where the law could hold him for trial on the charge of attempted murder.

He had drawn the sheriff's teeth, but the more dangerous wolf was still at large. Jasey had taken fright and fled the scene of the fiasco. Or at least he had chosen to avoid a meeting with Donal. He would want time in which to gather fresh forces for a last and decisive blow. Now that Circle C was on the warpath, the scheming lawyer would realize that a swift showdown was inevitable. He had to pluck the lightning from the clouds or he was a doomed man.

If Bearcat's hunch was right, Ruth Merrill was again in Jasey's hands. To think of the possibilities was unbearable torture.

Donal resolutely kept his mind from dwelling on them. Unbridled and terrifying imaginings would only weaken him. For the sake of the girl he loved he must keep his emotions under tight leash. He was going to need all his strength, mentally and physically. Where ruthlessness was needed, he would be ruthless . . . he must match cunning with greater cunning. He could not afford to let the gaunt spectre of fear disarm him.

Sagebrush and piñons and junipers dropped behind him. The trail left the boulder-strewn floor of the canyon and twisted through a scattering of oaks that presently gave way to tall yellow pines and suddenly Donal saw the landmark for which he was looking—the lofty and rugged crags of Eagle Peak.

He could hear the muted roar of the falls in the plunge down to Eagle Creek. The thirsty horse flung up his head, twitched eager ears and broke into a fast lope.

The trail, level here, cut between low hills and dropped down to a wide mountain meadow fringed with giant Ponderosa pines. He glimpsed an antlered buck in graceful flight, and memories of other visits to Injun Meadows came—and hurt. He used to come to the meadows with his father, and old Rusty Cross. They could always find deer, and sometimes bear and mountain lions. He had killed his first bear here. His fourteenth birthday, and he had killed the bear with his new rifle—a present from Rusty. He still had that rifle. He would like to use it on the man who had shot Rusty in the back.

Again he resolutely returned his mind to the grim present. It was necessary to keep his mind clear. His one thought now must be Ruth Merrill. Ruth was depending on him. Her voice pressed on him, urgent, appealing. She was calling to him in her time of great peril.

It was not his intention to reach the Daker ranch until after dark. He could make it from the meadows in less than two hours and cache the horse near the creek that skirted the corral—the mesquite thicket where he had first met Ruth Merrill that early morning of his own escape. He would need the covering darkness. Later, there would be a moon, but by that time they would be well on the way back to Injun Meadows. They would camp at the meadows until early dawn. Daylight was needed for the dangerous descent of Rubio Canyon.

He pulled off the saddle, and after watering the horse in the creek shallows, put him on a rope to browse the short, nourishing grass. He had an hour's time to kill and it was a chance for Stormy to have a good feed.

He got his sandwiches from the saddle and

sprawled out on the grass, his back against a sun-warmed boulder. A pair of eagles were soaring above the lofty peak. He found himself grinning. He had once tried to climb that peak and find the nest. Rusty had had to rescue him from a ledge. It was on that same fourteenth birthday. Rusty had bawled him out for risking his neck. He had explained to Rusty that he wanted to get an eaglet from the nest and train it to ride on his wrist like the pictures he had seen in an old book. He was going to teach his eagle to hunt rabbits. Rusty had gruffly told him it was a fool notion. He could get all the rabbits he wanted with his new rifle. Donal remembered how his father and Rusty got into a heated argument about it. Rusty had stubbornly refused to believe that men had ever ridden to the chase with hawks on their wrists. A rope and a gun was all any man needed, and to prove his assertion he got his rope on a black bear that came prowling around the camp. The bear got away from him, carried off Rusty's pet rawhide reata. He was wild about it, and spent all the next day trailing the bear. He got the bear, and his rope, only this time he used his rifle.

Donal finished his sandwiches and reached for tobacco sack and papers. He slowly shaped the cigarette, his expression grim. He knew that he was deliberately forcing his thoughts away from the girl at the Daker ranch. He was in a fever of impatience to be in the saddle again. It was the hardest thing he ever did. Sitting there, waiting—trying not to think of what might be happening to the girl. The dragging minutes were hours of agony. He had to keep his mind away from the Daker ranch, think of other things, like eagles, bears—old Rusty. But thinking of Rusty brought the whole dreadful business full tilt into his mind. Rusty was part of it. Rusty was dead, murdered. His murderers held Ruth in their power. In spite of himself, the circle worked back to her.

He stared gloomily across the meadow at the tall yellow pines. When the sunlight left their tops he would be on his way.

Doggedly, grimly reining his impatience, he sat there. The pile of cigarette stubs grew. Three crows flew in from across the creek, made raucous protests at the sight of the intruders and winged away.

The sunlight was gone from the pines. Shadows started the evening crawl across the meadow. Donal reached for his saddle gear and went quickly to the horse.

The old Apache trail was an easy descent into the west fork of the Aliso. The black horse, rested and replenished, rocked along through the deepening twilight. The pine trees became dark shapes, merged into the blanket of the night that gradually enveloped hillside and gorge. Stars glimmered shyly, put on their scintillating splendor.

The trail leveled across a wide mesa densely covered with gnarled piñons. A big owl rose from a stump and took off in soundless flight. A coyote barked from somewhere in the depths of the canyon beyond the mesa.

They left the piñons behind and started down the trail that looped to the canyon floor. It was pitch dark now. Only the winking stars overhead. Donal let the horse take his time.

He turned his memory inside out, stripped from it all the details he could recall about the sprawling old ranch house. He knew every room of that house, every closet and passage. One year, when he was a small boy, his father and mother had taken a long trip to New York and he had stayed with old Jim Daker. Memories flowed back. He could find his way about in the dark in that house. There were things he knew that perhaps would have surprised even Ruth Merrill. The secret tunnel that led from the old tankhouse with its always creaking windmill. It was a certainty that Gober knew nothing of its existence. The underground passage from the tankhouse into the bedroom had always been Jim Daker's closely-guarded secret. He had shown it to Donal one day during that long visit. Donal had solemnly promised never to tell. He never had. He felt the promise was now going to pay a rich dividend.

The bedroom, which was on the ground floor,

had been Jim Daker's. The windows on one side overlooked the high-walled garden. Also there was a door that led out to a veranda. Other windows looked out on a grove of cottonwoods that reached beyond the avenue.

Donal was sure that Colonel Merrill would have been occupying this room. But the colonel was dead, and it was entirely possible that Jasey would be using it, now that the ranch was his headquarters. He hoped fervently that Jasey was a man who went to bed very late. He wanted that room to be empty if he were going to make use of the secret tunnel.

Getting into the house unobserved was only a small part of the problem. He would have to locate which of the bedrooms upstairs was Ruth's. His recollection of the upstairs favored the room directly above the downstairs bedroom. It had the same view of garden and trees against a background of mountains. Ruth would be almost sure to have chosen this room among all the others. He recalled, too, that it had its own bath, which added to its desirability.

The chances were slim, Donal grimly reflected. He could think of no better plan, and anything was better than doing nothing. If the worst came, he would get Jasey first, and Gober, too. He would make sure of that.

The thought of failure sent a chill through him. He must not fail. For her sake he must put the possibility out of his mind. Her life, and more, depended on his making sure there could be no failure. It meant that he must use all the Indian stealth and cunning he had picked up from his father, from old Jim Daker and Roderick Dhu. *He had to get Ruth Merrill out of that house.*

He left the horse concealed in the bushes on the slope above the creek and slipped cautiously through the darkness toward the corrals. His first job was to get a horse for the girl, have it ready for the escape.

As silent as a ghost he reached the small corral in the rear of the barn. He could see the vague shapes of horses in the adjoining corral. Startled snorts drew him to a standstill. A commotion would bring men from the bunkhouse.

He stood motionless until satisfied he was no longer the object of suspicious attention, then quietly drew the gate open and crossed over to the barn's rear door which was already open.

It was hard to see a thing in that blackness. He stood for several moments, accustoming his eyes. Fortunately the door at the opposite end of the long line of stalls was open, and gradually he became able to distinguish objects.

A saddle hung on a peg almost within touch of his hand. He quietly lifted it down, made sure of the bridle, and then turned his attention to the horse munching in the stall opposite the peg. He spoke softly, reached for the tie-rope and backed the animal out.

In less than a minute he was out of the barn, the saddle slung over a shoulder and the horse following on the lead-rope.

He reached the creek and halted long enough in the willows to saddle and bridle the horse. Choosing an animal from the long line in the stable had been a gamble. He had laid hold of the nearest to his hand and had been lucky. The horse was gentle and willing, a brown, or dark bay. Donal could not be sure in that blackness. He knew horses, and the feel of this one under his hands told of sturdy, clean-built lines. The horse could run, if it came to a race.

Hugely satisfied, he stepped into the saddle and forded the creek and in a few minutes had his find cached with Stormy in the bushes.

He had made a good start, but he refused to let the uplift of strengthened hope lessen his caution. Stealthily, soundless as a stalking Apache, he crawled through the brush, skirted wide of the corral to avoid the horses and finally reached a clump of trees that loomed up in the black night behind the bunkhouse.

Lamplight glowed from a window, a pale golden rectangle in that darkness. He could hear the murmur of voices, and from the exclamations and muttered curses, it was evident that a poker game was in progress.

He stood there for long moments, carefully checking his next move. He wished he dared open the corral gate and send the horses into the pasture—the same with the animals in the barn. The plan had a serious drawback. He knew the way of horses. They would stampede from that corral in a mad ecstasy of delight. The noise of their drumming hoofs would instantly sound the alarm, bring men tumbling from the bunkhouse hot foot.

Abandoning the idea, he moved to the next clump of trees, a vague shape that made no sound. He could see the house, now. Lamplight flowed from the downstairs windows. The upper windows, those he could see, were dark.

The flare of disappointment in him passed as he realized that he was on the wrong side of the house for a view of the two bedrooms that interested him. He must work his way into the cottonwood grove. The windows faced that way, also overlooked the walled garden. The cottonwood grove would give him the best view.

He lingered to study the approach to the tankhouse. It loomed up in the night, a square, massive structure, separated by some ten yards from the kitchen quarters. The first floor was used as a dairy, the second held the huge ten thousand gallon tank, and crowning the building was the windmill tower.

Donal had been all over the place, and up in

the tower. Old Jim Daker would let him oil the windmill with its huge whirling fans. It was working now at a fast rate under the freshening night wind. Judging from its creaks and groans it had not been oiled for a long time.

Donal had been hoping for those creaks and groans. They would cover any noise he might accidentally make in the tankhouse. It would be dark as pitch in there.

He crept cautiously past the kitchen and came to the high wall that enclosed the garden. He kept on, thankful for the protecting wall, the added darkness, and suddenly he was around the corner and slipping like a ghostly shadow into the cover of the big cottonwoods.

His first quick glance at the house set his heart pounding. Lamplight gleamed in the windows of the corner room upstairs. Ruth's room, if his guess was correct.

His look went to the room below. The windows there were dark. It meant that Jasey was either not at the ranch, or that he was in the big living room that opened out on the patio. A faint glow beyond the high walls indicated a light in the living room. Jasey was there. The light proved he was.

Donal's eyes narrowed thoughtfully. A new plan was shaping in his mind. If he could get at Jasey without raising the alarm, get Jasey under his gun, it would simplify things. He could tie him up, gag him and be a long way on the road toward home with Ruth before Jasey's plight was discovered. It would probably be daylight before anybody suspected anything wrong. The horse would be missed from the barn and the news carried to Jasey who would then be found—missing.

Missing. Jasey found missing! Donal's pulse quickened. Why not? He could force Jasey to accompany them. His disappearance would be a complete mystery to Gober. And coupled with the girl's disappearance, Gober might even think that Jasey himself had carried her away in the dead of night. Gober would be a very puzzled man. He would do a lot of conjecturing, but never get within a hundred miles of the truth.

It was a crazy idea. Donal realized it instantly. His one and only job was to get Ruth Merrill away. It was folly to think of anything else. Her life was at stake, and more.

He continued to study that faint glow above the garden wall. The first part of the idea was sound enough. If Jasey was alone in that room, the chances to get a gun on him were good. Once he had him tied up and gagged, tucked out of sight in some closet, the rest of it would be not too difficult. He could have Ruth on her horse within the next fifteen minutes.

Something seemed to move out there, in the darkness near the garden gate. Cold prickles chased up and down his spine. The next instant the challenging bark of a dog shocked his ears.

A door slammed, and Donal heard a man's loud voice, the quick pound of booted feet on the porch. He reached for his gun.

17

Alamo checked his horse and fixed far-sighted eyes on the object that had caught his roving gaze. It gleamed from a clump of sagebrush, perhaps an old tin can, or the whitened bone of some long dead animal. Or it might be something else—a sign that Ruth Merrill had passed this way.

The old mountain man was an experienced trailer. Long years in the remote places had bred in him a canny instinct. He had learned never to ignore what he did not understand. It was second nature for him to investigate the thing that glinted in the clump of sagebrush.

He marked the clump carefully. That tiny gleam was reflected sunlight. It would be easy to lose sight of it, once he moved from his present position. One clump of sagebrush was discouragingly like another.

Satisfied he had the location safely established, he rode slowly toward the clump, leading the bay mare he had brought for Ruth. As he expected, the gleam vanished. He was not worried. It was only necessary to keep the clump in direct line with the red butte some fifty yards behind it.

He reached the spot, climbed from his saddle

and peered carefully at the dusty gray-green branches. He grunted, reached into the branches and disentangled a crumpled white Stetson. A silver buckle adorned the leather band.

Alamo stood there, turning the hat thoughtfully in his hands, his face grave. He knew that hat. He had himself hand-carved that leather band for Ruth Merrill's new Stetson, and he had hammered out the silver buckle from a piece of virgin silver.

"Got blowed into the bresh when she lost it in the sandstorm," he muttered.

He gazed about searchingly, trained eyes studying the terrain. The chances were against the hat traveling far after being swept from its owner's head. The brush was thick, and the hat would be quickly trapped, held tenaciously by the clawing branches. The wind had driven this one deep into the sagebrush. It could have lain there for years unnoticed, had it not been for the flash of sunlight on silver buckle, and Alamo's hawk eyes—his ability to read a message in trifles that other men would pass by.

He left the horses and circled the bush, head bent in a close study of the ground. He moved slowly, pausing frequently to scrutinize the bushes, any soft earth, even the stones that might show faint scratches from stumbling feet.

Gradually he widened the circle, never for an instant relaxing his attention, and suddenly he froze to a standstill, stood staring at the faint imprints under his eyes.

Carefully noting the direction taken by the wearer of those small, high-heeled boots, Alamo hung the white Stetson on a scraggly greasewood branch to mark the spot and with a satisfied grunt went with his long, loose-jointed stride back to the waiting horses.

In the saddle again, he recovered the hat and slowly followed the faint imprints left by Ruth Merrill's stumbling feet.

He saw where sudden fright had made her leap back from the big greasewood and correctly guessed the reason.

"Seed a rattler," he muttered. "Jumped most a yard, from the way her heels dug in."

Compassion was in his deep-set eyes as he followed the trail left by those faltering, weary feet. He came to the ridge, and dismounting from his horse, climbed out to the ledge. No footprints here, on the hard stone, but something else that proved beyond doubt that she had stood here, gazing into the canyon below.

Alamo stared for long moments at the faint impression made in the soft earth that clung to the roots of a piñon where Ruth had placed her hand for support in her climb down to the ledge. The freshness of the imprint told him he was not far behind her. Perhaps two hours—not more than three.

The old mountain man straightened his long, gaunt frame and gazed somberly into the canyon. There would be water there. She would be needing water.

There was no smoke lifting above the trees, but his keen eyes, trained for details, were quick to read the signs. The black object he glimpsed through the branches was a stovepipe, and a stovepipe meant a cabin. He would find her down there in that cabin.

Alamo scrambled up from the ledge and hurried with long strides to the horses. He was unaware that the words he was muttering were a prayer wrung from the innermost depths of him.

It took him nearly half an hour to reach the floor of the canyon. A man on foot could have made it in half the time, but there were sheer drops impossible for a horse, and Alamo had two of them to get down.

He bitterly begrudged the time, but he could not leave them behind. He was going to need horses. The girl would be in no shape for any more walking in that rough country.

They were down at last, the cabin in full view a hundred yards away. Jerking hard on the lead-rope, Alamo got the horses into a gallop.

Almost before he was down from the saddle he sensed that something was wrong. The door of the cabin was open, but there were no signs of life there.

Alarm grew in him. The girl had not found her way to the cabin. She was not here, or else she had been and gone. Or worse still . . . she had collapsed—was lying in there—dead.

He went slamming into the cabin and came to an abrupt standstill. His heart sank into his boots. The place was empty.

He swung back to the door, halted and stared at the stove. The lingering smell of recently-cooked bacon was enough to tell him that somebody had been in the cabin, and not long before his own arrival.

Alamo reached the rusty stove in two strides. The ashes in the grate were still warm.

He stood there, frowning gaze slowly moving around the little room. The cabin had been used as a temporary camp, he realized. An empty whiskey bottle lay on the rickety table. Another bottle lay shattered in a corner where it had been flung.

The old mountain man was not liking the signs. The cabin was a hideout for lawless men, border desperados who would have no respect, no pity for a girl like Ruth Merrill. The thought of what might have happened drew a despairing groan from him.

He had to make certain, satisfy himself that she had not innocently blundered into this lonely and sinister place, thinking to get help, but finding only wolves in human shape.

Grimly patient now, he began a fresh search of the room, bent down low for a closer study of the scuffed tracks. He soon found what he dreaded to see. The imprints of her little boots stood out sharp, and from the length of the stride he knew she had been running when she made them. His eyes followed them across the floor, to the window darkened by the thick-growing bushes outside. She had been standing near the window, and something had frightened her, and she had run outside.

Alamo's stooping frame sagged despondently. He had seen a lot of grim tragedies in his long life. He was toughened and hardened to death and disaster. This thing was a nightmare that would haunt him to his dying day. He would never again so completely taste the bitter dregs of despair.

He turned away from the window, halted again, eyes fixed on a crumpled and soiled little handkerchief under a broken-backed rawhide chair. He picked it up, straightened it out on the palm of his big hand. The initials, *RM*, were embroidered in one corner.

Alamo glanced briefly at the pan of water on the table. The handkerchief was still slightly damp. She had used it to wash the dust from her face. It had slipped from her hand and fallen under the chair. She would not be thinking of handkerchiefs at that moment.

He slowly tucked the bit of cambric in a

pocket, and stared with narrowed eyes at the patch of sunlight beyond the door. The yellowing light warned of approaching night. He must do something—not stand there letting despair clog his brain.

Grim purpose blazed up in his eyes. He went swiftly outside, and like an eager hound nosing a hot scent, he followed Ruth's tracks around the side of the cabin and back again to the doorstep, and then on to the point under the tree where she had waited for Ben Ferrel to bring the horses from the corral.

He studied the scuffed tracks, a man's big boots, the girl's smaller imprint, the hoof marks made by the horses. Two horses. It was from this tree that the man and the girl had ridden away.

Renewed hope put a leap into his pulse. The girl had suffered no harm—yet. She had ridden away with a lone man. She could be on her way back to the ranch—or she could be a *prisoner*.

Alamo thought of the footprints in the cabin. She had fled from the place in terror.

He shook his head somberly. The girl was not being taken back to the ranch. She was a helpless prisoner. He felt it in his bones.

A frenzy of energy drove him now. He swung up to his saddle and hurried the horses to the spring below the cabin. The animals must be watered before he took up the pursuit, and he would refill the canteen.

He slid down again from the saddle and snatched at the canteen. His reaching hands went rigid. Something was swaying from the end of a rope under the big cottonwood near the corral.

Alamo's eyes showed no horror, only grim curiosity. Dead men hanging from trees were no novelty. Most of them had well earned the rough justice of the times.

He left the horses to drink their fill and went for a closer look. The dead man was a stranger, a Mexican, and as he looked at the dangling corpse a possible explanation hit him like a blow. This dead man was the missing Pasqual Torres.

Alamo wrinkled his brows worriedly. If his guess was right, the finger pointed straight at Anse Jasey—at Gober. The cabin was the gang's secret hideout and it meant that Ruth Merrill was again in their clutches. She was being hurried to Rocking D—back to the man who had murdered her father.

The mountain man spun sharply on his heel, halted with a muttered exclamation.

"Effen he *is* the Torres hombre, 'tain't right to leave him swingin'."

He reached a long Bowie knife from inside his belt and slashed the rope, caught the lifeless body and lowered it gently to the ground.

What to do with the body had him puzzled for a moment. He disliked leaving it on the ground. The buzzards would flock to a feast the next day.

Alamo scowled. He was in a fever of impatience to be on his way. No dead man that ever was must delay the pursuit. Ruth Merrill's danger was a very real thing. And yet . . . this dead man might be Pasqual Torres, with a long record of loyal service to Circle C.

He lifted the lifeless body into his arms and almost ran with it to the cabin and stretched it out on the table. At least he could give Donal an accurate description of him. Small, youngish, a trim black mustache, the end of a little finger missing. He might be Pasqual. Alamo didn't know. He had never laid eyes on the son of Marica Torres.

He closed the door, hooked it against the wind and hurried back to the horses. His plans were already made. No use attempting to follow the trail. He would point straight for Rocking D. If he could hit the Aliso Creek trail at the forks before dark he would have a chance to read sign. He would know if the lone rider and his helpless prisoner had preceded him.

His long, gaunt frame swaying easily in the saddle, the old mountain man kept his horse moving at a brisk lope. The bay mare trotted freely alongside. Alamo was pleased with her. He had fretted at the thought of losing time with a led horse. He would have had to turn her loose if she had been inclined to drag on the lead-rope.

He pushed on steadily through the never-ending sagebrush, a grizzle-bearded, fierce-eyed old man, and the steady beat of pounding hoofs lifted his heart. He would make it. *He had to make it.*

18

The wind drift was with them and they rode in a haze of dust. Ruth made ineffectual attempts to clear her inflamed eyes. Despite her pleadings, Ferrel had tied her wrists loosely to the saddle horn and she could lift her hands barely high enough to touch her face.

Her lips were dry and sore. She was sore all over, and her head ached miserably. She had never felt so at the end of things.

Ferrel made no effort at conversation. His red bandanna was drawn up over his mouth against the dust, and his hat pulled low to break the glare of the sun now a shimmering disk above the mountains. He seemed indifferent to her discomfort, the dust, the blinding sun in her eyes.

He had kept the horses moving at a steady jog for endless miles. She began to recognize familiar signs that told her they were nearing the Aliso Creek fork. They would soon be at Rocking D.

The thought appalled her. It was too cruel. Her flight that wet morning with Don Cameron and old Alamo had gone for nothing.

It came to her miserably that she had only herself to blame. Donal had asked her to be careful, stay close to the ranch. She was getting what she deserved.

The ease with which her thoughts turned to Donal had ceased to make her wonder. The thing had happened that anxious morning when he appeared out of the mist with old Alamo.

She could still see the curious half wonder in him as their eyes met for the first time. The impact of his look had profoundly stirred her. Something had passed between them at that moment. She was aware of it now, and so was he. Which made this thing all the more horrible.

The sun was sinking fast. Its tip showed above the ridge like a sliver of blinding steel. Ferrel broke his long silence.

"Can make it easy before dark," he said.

Ruth did not even look at him. She hated him.

"Jasey's goin' to be mighty glad to see you ridin' into the yard," Ferrel grinned.

"I could kill you," Ruth said fiercely.

The man laughed. "Wildcat, huh? Jasey'll tame you, time he gits done with you."

The sneer in his voice jolted her pride, stiffened waning courage. Her head turned in a blazing look at him. "You're a pack of cowards! I'm not afraid of you."

"Big talk," he jeered. Suddenly he was crowding her horse off the trail. Her heart turned over. He leaned from his saddle and she felt the hard press of his gun against her side.

"No noise!" he whispered harshly.

The threat of instant death held her stiff with

terror. It was hard to be brave at that moment. Death finished everything, but hope did not entirely die while life remained.

The moments dragged. Something stirred in the brush that concealed them from the trail. She glimpsed the half-breed's vicious face.

She felt the press of the gun relax. Ferrel, plainly surprised, spoke curtly.

"What is it?"

Squint's face wore a curious grin. He thumbed at the girl. "Ain't talkin' till you've tied her mouth up," he said.

Ferrel eyed him sharply, nodded acquiescence and hastily slipped the red bandanna from his neck. The half-breed snatched it from him and moved close to the girl's horse. Ferrel's gun again jabbed her side. She made no resistance, let the man knot the bandanna over her mouth. It smelled strongly of sweat and dust and tobacco.

Squint stepped back, nodded satisfaction with his work and gave the other man a crafty grin. "Was scared she'd mebbe start yellin' if her mouth wasn't tied," he said.

"What for would she yell?" Ferrel asked, impatiently.

"That Alamo hombre is layin' in the bushes back in the fork," the half-breed told him. "I spotted him from down in the lower trail. Seen him ride out of the east fork with another bronc on a lead-rope."

Ferrel muttered an oath. *"Alamo!"* He flung a furious look at the girl. "All set to pull off an ambush, huh . . . git the gal away from us, huh?"

The half-breed's grin was wicked. "We'll spoil his play."

"You're damn right we'll spoil his play," growled the other man. His eyes narrowed thoughtfully. "Where's the Mex?"

"Staked him out in the bushes, along with the broncs. Figgered you wasn't far behind and headed back on foot to cut your trail."

There was a long silence, while Ferrel digested the news and laid his plans. Ruth watched him over the smelly bandanna that covered her face to the eyes. Her thoughts raced desperately. Alamo had picked up the trail, had made a shrewd guess and ridden to intercept them at the Aliso Creek fork. Luck had gone against him, and now they would kill him. The ambush he planned was a death trap for himself. The half-breed was right in his insistence that they gag her. She would have screamed a warning, screamed with all the power of her lungs. Her helplessness enraged her. She could do nothing to warn the stanch old man. It was more than she could bear. Alamo dead, and all because of her own folly.

She watched the unlovely pair with imploring eyes while they discussed the best way to surprise the man lying in wait for them. Squint was in favor of stalking the ambush.

"Sneak up on him and fill him full of lead," Squint said. "He won't have a chance to pull trigger."

Ferrel shook his head. "That old-timer can hear a wood-tick crawl in the dark. He's got Injun ears and eyes. We wouldn't know he'd spotted us till his gun got to smokin'. I ain't facin' that hombre with a gun in his hand."

"You're the boss," grumbled the half-breed.

Ferrel grinned. "I've got a play that'll have him plenty fooled. I'll ride along with the gal like I didn't know he's layin' there. He'll git his gun on me. I'll act scared as hell, let him take my gun and climb down from my saddle. He'll think the play's over and start tyin' me up. You come along and git the drop on him."

"He'll likely start pullin' trigger when he sees you headin' into the fork," argued Squint.

"Not with the gal so close to me," Ferrel said. "He won't risk hurtin' her."

"Nothin' to stop him from fillin' you with lead when he gits your gun away," persisted Squint, still dubious. "He won't wait to tie you up."

"Alamo ain't made that way," Ferrel said, confidently. "He's a tough hombre, but he ain't got the killin' instinct, like me and you." His tone indicated deep contempt for what he considered Alamo's weak spot.

They made certain that the bandanna was fastened securely. An untimely warning from the girl would find them facing a man whose gun could spell death with lightning accuracy.

With her horse close-held on the lead-rope, Ferrel jogged slowly up the trail. He knew that the half-breed was pacing him in the chaparral. Squint had ghost feet, a way of making himself invisible.

Ruth thought wildly of throwing herself from her saddle. She would be dragged to death, but the commotion would spoil Ferrel's cunning ruse to surprise the unsuspecting Alamo. She abandoned the idea as useless. Alamo would be certain to run to help her. They would shoot him down.

Ferrel swung into the down-trail fork, careful to keep Ruth's horse stirrup to stirrup with his. The man in ambush would have no chance to get in a shot without danger to the girl.

Ruth held her breath, her heart in her mouth, and suddenly a low, drawling voice broke the twilight stillness.

"Hold it, Ferrel. I've got you covered."

Ferrel checked his horse with a well-simulated grunt of surprise. His hands shot up, submissively.

Alamo stepped into view, his seamed face as grim as death. A long stride carried him close to Ferrel's horse. He waggled the Colt in his hand gently. "Climb down."

Ferrel grinned, slid from the horse. He kept his

hands up, his back to the old mountain man. He knew that Alamo would never bring himself to shoot a man in the back.

"I'm tying you up," Alamo said. "I mebbe should kill you right now. I jest ain't your kind of murderer." He reached for the rope coiled on Ferrel's saddle.

Ruth watched, fascinated, horrified, her heart like lead. She managed a gurgling sound that Alamo quite misunderstood.

He flung her a pitying look. "Sure, Ruthie—I'll have you loose jest as soon as I git this wolf tied up good."

He slowly holstered his gun and with a quick motion dropped a noose over Ferrel's lifted hands. And then, soundless as a jungle beast stalking its prey, the half-breed glided from the bushes. The girl's strangled, animal-like moan swung Alamo's head in a quick look at her. Dismay leaped into his eyes, his jaw sagged.

The half-breed said, softly, "Git away from him, Ben. I'm unloadin' this gun on him right now."

Ferrel flipped the noose from his wrists and faced cautiously around. He had different ideas. There was a picture in his mind, a triumphant return to Rocking D. The capture of Ruth and Alamo would put him high in Anse Jasey's favor.

He said, curtly, "No gunplay, Squint."

"Huh?" Squint's surprise was genuine. "You're loco. No sense takin' him to the ranch."

Ferrel gave him an ugly look. The half-breed's fool talk had been annoying him of late. Some day soon he'd have to fix Squint . . . make dead meat of him. He said, raspingly, "I ain't arguin'—"

He reached for Alamo's gun, jabbed it against the old man's spine. "Git his horse," he said to Squint. "Soon as we git him in his saddle we'll rope him." He glanced briefly at Ruth. "You can take that bandanna off her mouth. Anse won't like it if her lips are cut bad." He grinned.

The callous gibe restored the half-breed's good humor. Leering obscenely he removed the gag and then vanished into the thicket in search of Alamo's horses.

Alamo gave the white-faced girl a look of mingled pity and shame. He broke his silence. "I was some careless, Ruthie. Thar ain't words bad enough to call me."

Her lips quivered, tears sprang to her eyes. "It's not your fault—"

"I'm right sorry, Ruthie—"

His self-abasement hurt her. "It's not your fault," she repeated, vehemently.

Ferrel interrupted them. "How come you cut our trail?" His pale bulging eyes interrogated Alamo.

"Waal, now—" Alamo was cautious with his

answer. It would make bad matters worse if these men knew he had followed the trail from their secret hideout in the canyon. They would realize he wouldn't have missed seeing the dead man hanging from the tree. To admit his knowledge would frighten them, and frightened men were prone to go to extremes.

He had no desire to precipitate an immediate crisis. A dead Alamo Jones would be of no use to Ruth Merrill in this time of peril. It was very necessary for him to keep on living, use every wile at his command that would hold life in his body.

Ferrel was eyeing him suspiciously. "How come you laid for us here?"

"Waal—" Alamo's tone was mild. "Got to figgerin' that mebbe the gal was out ridin' this way. Her horse showed up and from the signs it seemed like she'd got throwed."

"So you come over here lookin' for her, huh?" Ferrel jeered.

"Sure warn't lookin' for *you,*" drawled Alamo. He managed a sheepish grin.

Squint brought up the horses. Alamo climbed back to his saddle and the two men quickly made him fast with the rope.

He gibed at them good-humoredly. "You fellers act like I was some dang'rous," he chuckled. "Ropin' my hands to the saddle . . . puttin' hobbles on me."

The half-breed jerked viciously at a knot. He was not in favor of all this trouble for a man who in his opinion was better dead.

"You'll be wearin' the rope for a necktie awful soon," he prophesied. "Al Gober will figger to dangle you for killin' Pete Starr on the ridge road."

"Now, Squint—" The old mountain man's voice was reproachful. "I'm gittin' right narvous—the way you talk."

The half-breed mounted the bay mare Alamo had so doggedly brought for the girl and vanished at a rapid pace down the trail. Ferrel followed with the prisoners, their horses on lead-ropes.

They overtook Squint at the lower fork. The half-breed had shifted back to his own horse and the mare was again on a rope.

Ruth stifled an exclamation as she recognized the tall Mexican bound to the third horse. It seemed that Pasqual Torres also was en route to Rocking D. At least he was still alive. They had not murdered him—yet.

Alamo, on the horse trailing her, eyed Squint's prisoner with frank interest. Another Mexican. He began to speculate about him, and about the dead man he had left lying on the table in the cabin. Perhaps he'd been mistaken about the latter's identity. Perhaps *this* man was Pasqual Torres.

He saw the girl's face looking back at him. Her lips silently formed words.

Alamo frowned, narrowed his eyes. The twilight was deepening. It was hard to see clearly.

Ruth tried again, and this time he got it. She was repeating the name over and over. *Pasqual Torres*. The tall Mexican was the missing Pasqual Torres.

Alamo wondered grimly about the dead man in the cabin. His guess had been wrong. Whoever the unfortunate stranger might be, he had met death at the hands of these men now hurrying them down the trail.

The old frontiersman's thoughts were gloomy indeed. He could not delude himself. The outlook was grim.

Darkness was stealing over the landscape when at last they rode up the avenue that wound between the cottonwoods. Remnants of twilight gave Ruth a glimpse of the ranch house between the trees. The place seemed to be in darkness. A wild hope sprang in her. Jasey was not there. It would mean a respite. Every hour gained offered opportunities to be snatched—used.

She gave Alamo a quick look over her shoulder. It was too dark for him to see the revitalized expression on her face. He did not need to see it. The uplift of her chin, the courageous tilt of her head told him enough. Something had excited her—caused her to grasp at fading hopes.

He, too, had noticed the dark house and come to the same conclusion about Jasey's absence. He was himself cheered, aware of tingling excitement. He had been more than dubious about the reception he was to get from Jasey and Gober. A rope and the nearest tree, and no time lost about it. No reason for them to wait.

Jasey's absence would mean a welcome delay. A man wasn't dead until he was dead. Alamo's tough old body straightened in the saddle. A man could do a lot if he hung on, refused to stay beaten.

He was given no chance to speak to the girl. Ferrel hurried her into the house by way of the kitchen door.

A fat man in a soiled apron sat at the table playing solitaire with a greasy deck of cards. Ruth had never seen him before. He gave her an interested glance.

"The boss ain't got back from where he's went to," he told Ferrel. "Him an' Gober both."

"You ain't tellin' me," rasped Ferrel. He was disgruntled. Jasey's absence had spoiled his triumphal entry into the yard. "Calico's already give me *that* news." Surprise was suddenly in his eyes as he looked at the man. "How come you got here? Thought you was ridin' herd on the hotel desk in town."

"I quit the job," the ex-hotel clerk said somberly. "I wasn't stickin' round, not after gettin' a look at that Don Cameron hombre." The fat man shook his head. "No, sir . . . not with *him* on the loose. You should have seen his eyes. Death in 'em. I cleared out . . . told the boss I'd ruther cook for you bunch of coyotes."

"You got the guts of a crawlin' worm," sneered Ferrel. He gestured impatiently. "Light me a lamp, feller. I'm hustlin' the gal up to her room."

The fat man took a lamp down from a shelf, lit it, and obeying Ferrel's gruff command, led the way into the hall and up the stairs.

He preceded them into the bedroom and placed the lamp on the dressing table. Ferrel looked at the girl uncertainly. "No call to leave you tied up," he said. "You ain't gettin' away from here ag'in."

He untied the cord from her wrists, removed the key from the door and motioned for the cook to follow him out.

Ruth heard his voice addressing the cook. "You're stickin' close to this door, savvy? The boss'll have your skelp if you let her git away."

"I gotta cook," she heard the man protest. "How are you fellers goin' to eat if I don't git back to the stove?"

"I'll send Calico up," Ferrel's voice replied. "Soon as he gits here you can do your cookin'."

The rasp of his spurs faded down the hall. Ruth sank into a chair. She was frightened, but thankful. It could have been worse, so *much* worse.

She wondered what they would do with Alamo, and poor Pasqual Torres. She had the comforting feeling that for the moment they, too, would not be harmed.

She wondered about Pasqual Torres. It was mysterious business. Pasqual—and the poor dead Mexican who was of course the Salvador Antista who had written the threatening letter to Mrs. Cameron. There seemed no other explanation. Pasqual's connection with him baffled her.

Heavy footsteps in the hall, the murmur of voices, informed her that Ferrel had sent Calico to relieve the cook from his post at the door.

She frowningly considered Calico. It was useless to appeal to him. He was as vile as the worst of them. He was the man Donal had tricked when he escaped from the granary. Calico would not be caught off guard a second time.

An hour passed. The fat cook brought her a bowl of beef stew on a tray, with bread and coffee. His leers offended her. She averted her face until he left the room.

She hated the thought of food, but forced herself to eat, found that she was ravenous. She was young, and healthy, and she had eaten nothing since early morning. Her last meal had been the bacon sandwich at the cabin.

The hours dragged. She lay on the bed, eyes wide open, ears keyed to every sound. It would not be long now. Jasey would be coming. The door would open, and she would see him standing there—see his smirking face, his hot, enfolding eyes.

Footsteps in the hall drew her from the bed in a panic. She backed away to the window, frightened eyes on the door. It opened. Jasey stepped inside, stood looking at her.

He was not smiling. His face wore a harassed expression, lips tight, eyes hard.

He said, "So you're back."

She found her voice, spoke fiercely. "I've been dragged back here like a runaway slave."

He shook his head reproachfully. "My dear girl—"

"Don't pretend!" she flared.

Jasey ignored the interruption. "Ferrel told me about it. You were lost, nearly out of your mind . . . in fact you were rather violent. He had a bad time of it, getting you home."

"While you are here, this is not my home," Ruth said. "I'm leaving at once, and don't you dare to keep my door locked—a man on guard."

Jasey looked injured. "It's for your own good." He regarded her intently. "I'm afraid you don't like me."

"I don't!"

"You may—given time—"

Ruth's eyes blazed. "Are you keeping me here against my will?"

"You're very tired," he said. "I suggest you get a good night's rest. We'll talk things over in the morning." His voice hardened. "It will pay you to be more cooperative, my dear." He drew a long envelope from his pocket and tossed it on the bed. "In the meantime, look this paper over. I'll want you to sign it."

"Suppose I refuse to sign it?"

His smile made her flesh creep. "You won't refuse, my dear. Not that it really matters." His eyes were like bits of shiny brown glass. "I'm a smart man, my dear."

The door closed gently behind him. She was alone again. Relief waved over her. More time granted. She could still continue to hope. She would not for one moment let go of hope.

She went to the bed and picked up the envelope. She might as well know what it was he was so sure she would sign.

She drew the folded document from the envelope and studied it with growing amazement. It appeared to be a quitclaim deed to the Daker ranch. Her father's signature was already on it. At least it closely resembled his signature. Ruth was convinced it was a forgery. Her father had never even hinted that he was selling Rocking D. There was a place for her own signature, relinquishing any claim she might have as the late Colonel Merrill's heir.

More incredible than even the purported signature of her father was the name of the man supposed to be buying the ranch.

Ruth's bewilderment grew. Salvador Antista was dead. She had seen his lifeless body hanging from a cottonwood tree. And yet his name was on the deed as purchaser.

Completely mystified, she tossed the paper back on the bed and returned to the opened window, drew in long breaths of the cool night air. It looked so peaceful, out there. The giant cottonwoods, a dark blur against the black night.

Her confused thoughts turned to Don Cameron. He would be looking for her. Don was clever. He was a man who put fear into other men. The very look in his eyes had terrified the fat cook. Don was like his father, they all said, and his father's name was legend in the Rio Seco country—and Don was like him.

Her gaze went desperately to the dark blur of trees. Surely he would come to her, know her need.

Of a sudden her heart seemed not to beat, and there was no breath in her. She looked again. She was not mistaken. Something moved under the cottonwoods—a vaguely-seen shape.

A dog suddenly set up an uproar.

Ruth clung to the sill, sick with apprehension. It was Don, out there, and the dog had given the alarm. She heard men—running.

19

Donal, flattened against the tree, heard the rustle of dry leaves. The dog rushed at him, circled off, barking furiously. A coyote yipped derisively from the chaparral across the road and, diverted by this new challenge, the dog gave chase at top speed.

The pounding footsteps halted. Donal heard a man's relieved voice. "Coyotes—"

"That damn pup goes loco every time he smells one," grumbled another voice. "He'll git to chasin' 'em too far some night and they'll sure chew him up."

The footsteps retreated up the path to the house. The screen door slammed.

Donal let out a relieved grunt. It was a lucky break. He had a tender feeling for coyotes at that moment. He would never again look at one over the barrel of a rifle. Circle C range was going to be sanctuary for the little prowlers from now on.

He holstered the gun and stared irresolutely at the house. No doubt about the first speaker. Anse Jasey. The other man was Al Gober. He had reason to remember that bleak voice. It was going to be hard to get at Jasey while Gober was with him.

Another, and more immediate problem, was

the dog. It would take some maneuvering to get inside the house without again attracting the dog's unwelcome attention. A second alarm, close in, would be fatal. It was obvious that Jasey was nervous. He was aware that the entire Circle C outfit would be searching for the girl and that the trail would eventually lead to the Daker ranch.

His alert ears caught the scuff of dry leaves behind him. He stiffened, slowly turned his head, saw a vague shape slithering toward him.

He racked his brain desperately for something he could do to silence the animal. Something that Gober had said flashed into his mind. Gober had spoken of the dog as a pup. A pup was apt to be friendly if given the chance.

Donal relaxed, spoke softly. "Hello, there." His tone was inviting.

The dog halted, cocked his head appraisingly, puppy-fashion. Donal saw that he was a half-grown sheep dog. He spoke again, offered a hand, and after a brief hesitation the pup slowly approached and cautiously sniffed at his legs. Apparently everything was all right. This stranger smelled of horses and saddle-leather and range dust. It was a good, honest smell, the pup decided. He wagged his tail, wriggled delightedly.

Donal grinned, rubbed the squirming dog's ears. He would have no more trouble with *this* rapturous friend.

His gaze went again to the lighted window

upstairs. He held his breath. The slender shape framed against the lamplight was Ruth. The alarm had aroused her. She was watching—hoping.

Donal moved swiftly, reached a little clearing directly below the window.

He took off his hat, waved it from side to side, hoping the motion would draw her eyes to him through the darkness.

The pup cocked inquisitive ears. The man was playing a game and he must do something to help the fun along. He whimpered, let out a plaintively demanding yelp.

Donal grabbed him, stood motionless, eyes on the window. The girl was leaning far out, and there was something fluttering in her hand. A handkerchief. She had seen him. The dog's stifled yelp had done the trick.

He waved again, got an answering signal, saw her turn quickly away.

It maddened him to be so near to her, and so helpless at that moment. He could not climb up to her, nor could she climb down, not without a ladder. An attempt to find a ladder in that darkness would bring down a hornet's nest.

He stood there, awaiting her return to the window, angrily aware that he was trembling. He must control his impatience, trample on doubts and fears. It was a time for coolness. The girl up there was depending on him.

The slender figure was back at the window and

signaling with the handkerchief. Donal waved his hat, saw a small object fly from her hand. It was a good throw, and the thing landed close to his feet. He picked it up, a small slipper attached to a line of stout sewing thread. He felt inside the toe, drew out a crumpled ball of paper.

Donal smoothed the paper open. It was impossible to read the note in the dark. He waved to indicate that he would be back and went stealthily into the deeper blackness of the grove. He found a small ditch, its banks overgrown with tall, concealing weeds, and sat on his heels, fumbling for matches.

Cupping the flame carefully he read the hasty scrawl. *Locked in room. Man outside door.*

The match flickered out. He did not bother to light another one. Straightening the piece of paper over a hard knee he found a pencil and scrawled his answer. *Wait—be ready.*

In less than five minutes he was back where the slipper lay in the grass. He broke the thread and tied the end to the piece of paper which he rolled into a spill. He stood up, signalled with his hat, one hand holding the pup as the paper danced away into the darkness. The dog whined, struggled to break loose and go in chase.

Donal stood there, clutching the dog, gaze on the girl in the lighted window. He could see the motions of her hands as she carefully drew the paper up the wall.

At last it was in her fingers. She unfolded the spill, head bent as she read his scrawl. He saw her face turn toward him and she held the paper up, nodding her head to let him know she understood.

He yearned to call up to her, hear her answering voice. It was hard to leave her, not knowing what the night would bring.

He followed the high patio wall and came again to the gate. The pup trailed sedately. He was not going to lose his new friend.

The animal was becoming a pest, a dangerous liability. Donal squatted on his heels and drew the dog to him. He had to make up his mind.

He drew his gun. A blow from the steel barrel would stun the animal, make him a very sick dog for several hours to come. He hated the thought, but there was so much at stake . . . Ruth—his entire world.

Donal set his teeth, lifted the gun, was suddenly aware of a moist tongue licking his fingers. He grinned, slowly pushed the gun in his holster. He couldn't do it. The dog trusted him.

He said, with a mingling of irritation and affection, "You damn little pup—"

He forced his mind to calm consideration of one plan after another. He again studied the possibilities of entering the house by way of the secret tunnel.

He was frankly dubious about the tunnel. Long

years had passed. He had no knowledge of its present condition. There was a chance he would find the passage hopelessly blocked.

Direct attack was the only alternative. He must wait until Jasey was alone, then act swiftly. In the meantime, he must get closer to the house, be ready the moment Gober left the room.

Avoiding the flagstones, Donal made a soundless approach to the wide veranda, moved like a shadow from bush to bush. The young sheep dog seemed to realize this was serious business and padded quietly at his heels. His forebears had for generations guarded flocks in the night. This man was his new master and needed his help.

Crouched under one of the windows, Donal listened to the low murmur of voices. Fortunately, the window was open. The words reached him distinctly.

"I'm for doin' the job right now." Gober's voice. He seemed to be in a grumbling, resentful mood. "No sense, takin' risks with them hombres."

"Tomorrow is soon enough." Jasey's voice indicated that his mind was not to be changed. "The girl's going to be stubborn. She'll sign fast enough when she sees those men standing under a tree with ropes around their necks. If she refuses to sign we'll swing them in front of her eyes."

"I reckon she'll sign quick enough," agreed

Gober. "She won't stand for seein' 'em jerkin' at the end of a rope."

There was a silence, and then Gober's voice again. Donal could picture the grin on his death's-head face. "Won't stop us from danglin' 'em, soon as she gits her name on that paper, huh?"

"You've guessed it." Jasey's voice was wicked with evil amusement.

"What do you figger to do with the gal, when things is settled?"

"It's going to be up to her," Jasey said. "She's a pretty piece. I could give her a good time, if she's sensible."

"She ain't made that way," Gober ruminated. "You'll have a wildcat on your hands."

"All the worse for her," Jasey said, venomously.

"Thar's places across the border." Gober told him with an obscene chuckle. "It's either that, or handin' her over to Squint. That damn half-breed is some crazy about her." He laughed again.

Donal heard the scrape of his chair. "Reckon I'll hit the hay, boss." Gober paused. "Them Circle C fellers will raise hell about her. I've got lookouts posted on the trails if they come nosin' round."

"They can't prove we know anything about her," Jasey said, confidently.

"Well, *buenas noches*—"

Donal heard the man's heavy footsteps, and then Jasey's voice.

"Wait a moment, Al." The lawyer's tone was thoughtful. "What you said about Squint has me thinking."

"Yeah?"

"We've got to fix young Cameron. Squint can have the girl . . . take her across the border and do what he wants with her if he gives Cameron the same dose of medicine he gave Rusty Cross. Cameron is too dangerous. With him out of the way, our troubles are over."

"I'd like to git that feller my own self," Gober said, savagely.

"I don't care who gets him, so long as it's done," purred the lawyer. "The years will roll back, Al. I'll come into my own, be king in this Rio Seco country. Circle C will be mine, and this Daker ranch. A cattle kingdom worth fighting for."

There was a long silence, and then Gober's voice, shaken, almost fearful. "I wouldn't want to be the man to stand in your way, Anse. I wouldn't want to be Don Cameron."

His footsteps faded down the hall. A door slammed softly—and then stillness. Only the wild yipping of a distant coyote.

The dog shivered against Donal's legs.

Donal waited, tense, ears alert. He wanted time to clear his confused mind. Who were the men they planned to hang in the morning? What did Jasey mean by his crazy talk? *The years will roll back . . . I'll come into my own, be king in the Rio Seco country.* The man was insane.

A noise in the room broke the stillness, the clink of a bottle against glass.

Donal took a cautious look. Jasey was in a big easy chair, his back to the window. He was pouring a drink from a whiskey bottle. He replaced the bottle on the table and leaned back in the chair, glass in hand. On the table was a gun, within easy reach.

It was going to be hard to effect a surprise entrance. An attempt to scramble through the window would give Jasey a perfect target for his gun.

Donal crouched there for a long moment, one hand on the dog's mane of hair, and it seemed to him that the idea took shape in those caressing fingertips, galvanized him to action.

He wanted to distract Jasey's attention from the veranda door. The pup was a heaven-sent means, would give him those desperately needed, precious moments.

The window was low and an active dog *could* make the leap. Jasey's suspicions would not be aroused. He would naturally think the dog had jumped into the room. At any rate his attention would be drawn to the window.

Donal seized the dog gently and, with a

quick motion, pushed him through the window. He heard Jasey's startled exclamation as the surprised dog landed on all fours—the scrape of Jasey's feet.

20

Donal did not wait to hear more. A few quick steps that made less sound than the wind in the trees brought him to the open door.

Jasey was on his feet and facing the window. It was plain that his scowling gaze frightened the dog.

He slowly replaced the gun he had snatched from the table and bent down, snapping his fingers. The pup rolled over on his back, waved apologetic paws.

Donal took a swift, noiseless step from the door. He said, softly, "Don't move, Jasey."

The words seemed to paralyze the man. He continued to crouch there, hand reaching out to the dog. A ghastly pallor waved into his dark face.

Donal spoke again, his low voice hardly above a whisper. "Don't speak . . . call for help, or I'll kill you."

The dog scrambled to his feet, whimpered uneasily.

Donal's harsh whisper leaped at him. "Quiet . . . Get in that corner."

The pup obeyed the gesture, curled up in the corner. This *was* serious business. His new master had a stern way that called for prompt obedience.

Donal wasted no time. He knew just what had to be done and how to do it in the quickest way. He jabbed his gun against Jasey's spine.

Obeying his whispered command, Jasey flattened face down on the floor. Fear of death had him trembling from head to foot.

Donal snatched a hair rope from an ornate silver-mounted saddle that hung on the wall. He drew Jasey's hands behind his back, lashed them tight, pulled the rope down and ran a double hitch around his ankles. He jerked the knots so tight that Jasey let out a groan. Donal rapped him on the head with the barrel of his gun.

"Do that again and I'll knock you senseless," he warned.

He rolled the man over on his back, found his handkerchief and balled it into his mouth. He needed something to make the gag secure and finally tore a long strip from the curtain billowing gently at an open window.

Donal stared down at his prisoner with grim eyes. The affair had consumed hardly five minutes. There had been no time for questions about the men condemned to be hung the next morning. His first duty was to get Ruth Merrill away from the house. Anything else must wait until he had the girl in a place of safety.

He recalled her brief message. A man was guarding her door.

His decision came swiftly. Only boldness could

help him now. The upstairs hall would be dimly lighted, the man unsuspecting.

His look went to the door that led to the downstairs bedroom. Jasey's, now. He bent down, gathered the helpless man in his arms and went in swiftly.

An idea put a hard grin on his face. He ripped the covers back, tumbled his prisoner on the bed and drew the covers over him.

He paused on his way out for a glance back at the bed, nodded grim satisfaction. Anybody chancing to look would think that Jasey was sound asleep under the covering blankets.

He slipped into the hall. The dog padded at his heels. Donal halted, indecisive for a brief moment. A faint smile touched his lips. He would let the dog follow him upstairs. The sight of the pup would reassure the man watching Ruth's door. The dog was a familiar sight around the house.

He went up the stairs, quietly, but not too quietly. He did not want any noise that would carry outdoors. But a too stealthy approach might alarm the guard.

He saw the dim light of a lantern on the hall floor, and a man, slumped in a chair tipped to the wall. A cigarette drooped from the corner of his mouth.

Donal approached him, hat pulled low over his face. The guard looked up sleepily, gave the dog a recognizing grin, and sent a longer, harder look at the man moving briskly toward him. "How come Jasey sent *you?*" He got out of the chair, stared at Donal with puzzled eyes. "Cain't see good in this light, feller. Thought it was Calico comin' back to relieve me."

"Calico found hisself a bottle an' got plenty soused." Donal stood, hands on hips, a grin on his shadowed face.

"Sure wish I could find *me* a bottle of the same stuff," snickered the man. He peered at Donal intently. "Ain't rememberin' seein' you before. Reckon you're the new jasper Al said was comin' from town."

"You're wrong," Donal drawled. His gun was suddenly against the man's ribs.

The guard gaped stupidly, slowly lifted his hands. He gave the dog an enraged look. "The pup knowed you," he stuttered. "Wasn't it Al as sent you up?"

"You're dumb from now on," Donal warned. "No more talk." He jerked the gun from the man's belt, gestured with it at the door. "Open—"

The dazed guard fumbled at the key with shaky hands. The lock clicked and he was reaching for the knob when the door jerked quickly open. Carried by the impetus, the man stumbled headlong into the room.

Ruth had no eyes for him. She stood there, hand clutching the doorknob, her gaze on the tall, grim-faced man in the shadowed hall.

He gestured for silence, stepped into the room and closed the door.

Ruth saw that haste drove him. She made no attempt to speak, took the confiscated gun he thrust at her and leveled it at the scowling guard.

Donal holstered his own Colt and gave her an admiring look. Her eyes were cool, her gun-hand steady.

He looked around for something that would serve to tie the captive. Ruth gestured at the bed. He grinned, seized the pieces of rope she had made ready for him. He wanted to hug her for the forethought, for her trust in his promise to come. Instead, he went to work with the pieces of rope.

He jerked the last knot tight, fashioned a gag with torn strips of towel and rolled the man out of sight under the bed.

Ruth broke her silence. "I used an old trunk cord," she said in a matter-of-fact voice. "I thought something like this would happen and that you'd want some rope handy."

Donal said nothing. He could only gaze at her, and then he was moving toward her, and she was moving toward him, and his arms were around her, drawing her close. Her hair was against his cheek soft, fragrant, and her lips when she lifted them to his were soft, too, and warm and generous with their sweetness.

He said, his voice husky, "I've died a thousand times—"

"I—I could have died, too—" Her voice was shaky. "Only—only I couldn't give up hope that—that you'd come."

He resolutely withdrew his arms from the slim, yielding waist. Danger stalked their every moment. The things he wanted to tell her must wait.

He said, curtly, "We haven't much time—" He drew his gun and turned to the door.

Ruth snatched up the gun she had dropped on the bed. She was fully dressed, even to the white Stetson that Alamo had found in the clump of sagebrush.

Donal opened the door, almost stumbled on the dog, crouching on the threshold, forlorn, whimpering. Donal had forgotten him, shut him out.

Ruth exclaimed, "Shep . . . it's Shep—"

Donal said, gravely, "You owe him a medal. He got me into this house—to you."

The pup flung himself at her, tongue lolling, eyes rolling in a frenzy of joy. Ruth stooped, hugged him. Shep broke from her, dashed at Donal and licked his hand.

"Quiet," Donal said, sternly.

Shep flattened his ears and went back to the girl, padded soberly at her heels as they made their way to the stairs and down to the hall.

In a few moments they were in the large ranch office. Donal closed the door, locked it and gestured for the girl to precede him through the veranda door.

Ruth came to an abrupt standstill, looked at him with troubled eyes. She had grown very pale.

"I—I forgot to tell you . . . everything has been so—so hectic—"

His eyes questioned her, impatiently. "We must get away from here," he said. "I've got horses waiting—across the creek—the place where we met that morning."

"You must listen," Ruth persisted. "Alamo is here—a prisoner." Her voice trembled. "He—he picked up my trail and followed—and—they caught him. They'll murder him—"

The expression on his face frightened her. She had never seen eyes so cold, so implacable.

He said, in a low, tight voice, *"Alamo?"*

Ruth nodded. "And Pasqual Torres—" She told him briefly of the rustler camp in the canyon and about the dead Mexican hanging from a tree.

He puzzled over the dead Mexican. "There's only one answer," he decided. "The man must have been Salvador Antista, though why Jasey's men should murder him is a mystery."

Ruth glanced at the bedroom door. Donal had told her while coming down the stairs of the brief encounter with Jasey.

"Couldn't you force him to release Alamo—and Torres?" She gestured at the door.

Donal shook his head. He was not going to risk her safety in a hazardous attempt to rescue Alamo and Torres.

"Too many of them," he said, sorrowfully. "Gober, Ferrel—a half dozen more, out in the yard, not counting the men Gober has watching the trails."

"I'll feel dreadfully all my life if—if we don't try to help—"

Donal regarded her unhappily, saw her eyes widen with alarm.

"Somebody in the hall," she whispered. "I saw the doorknob turn."

Donal hurled himself at the door, turned the key and ran into the hall. He was in time to glimpse a man, bootless, and clad only in red flannel underclothes, vanish into the kitchen.

Jerking gun from holster, Donal raced in pursuit. Ruth followed, hand clutching the revolver taken from the guard.

She dashed into the kitchen, in time to see the fleeing man snatch at a rope that dangled from the ceiling. Donal leaped at him, gun lifted. She saw the man's face, fat, fear-contorted. He jerked convulsively at the rope. Ruth's aghast ears heard the clang of a bell. It pealed a second time, and then Donal's gun barrel crashed against the man's skull. He crumpled senseless to the floor.

Donal looked at the white-faced girl. They were in for it now.

He seized her hand, hurried her toward the hall door.

21

Something beat at Ruth's brain as they ran out of the kitchen. A memory, elusive—important . . . *very* important. Something about the old ranch bell.

"Wait—" She spoke breathlessly, hung back against the pull of his hand. "Donal—that bell . . . it rang only twice—"

He sensed the urgency in her, halted reluctantly. "The bell?"

"Yes—" Ruth's hand tightened over his. "He only had time to ring it twice, and two rings mean the foreman is wanted at the house. Father used to ring the bell twice when he wanted Gober to come to the office."

Donal muttered an exclamation and was suddenly hurrying into the kitchen. He knew all about ranch bells. There was one at Circle C. The signals at Circle C were different. Two quick bells meant a summons for the boss, and three bells always a call for Rusty Cross. A continued pealing of the bell would bring the entire outfit on the run. The bell could be heard for miles.

He bent over the unconscious cook. The face was familiar. He had last seen this fat man behind the desk in the lobby of the Daker House.

There was no time to lose. Gober would soon

make an appearance if Ruth was right about two bells being his signal.

Ruth ran up, breathless, but cool. "I'll help," she said, and bent over the man's legs.

Between them they dragged the inert body across the floor and rolled it out of sight behind a closet door. Donal motioned to the girl and they slipped into the hall and back to the office.

He gave the girl a grim smile. "We'll soon know if you're right."

Ruth lifted a warning hand. "He's coming—"

Donal gestured at the bedroom door. "Quick—in there."

The girl hesitated only an instant. She was reluctant to leave, but realized her presence would distract him. She nodded, and, gun in hand, went swiftly across the room.

The door had hardly closed behind her when Donal heard the quick tread of booted feet.

He crouched behind the partly open door, gun lifted.

Gober stepped into the room. He wore a long-sleeved undershirt. Apparently he had been in bed and stopped only long enough to slip into trousers and boots.

He paused a moment, puzzled gaze on the empty desk chair.

"Sure thought I heard that damn bell ring," he muttered.

He came further into the room, halted with a

startled grunt as he felt the jab of Donal's gun in his back. His head turned slowly in an amazed look at the man behind him.

There was no gun on him. Gober had not expected trouble when he obeyed the familiar double clang of the bell. The incredulity in his eyes faded. They took on a glassy look.

He said, quietly, bitterly. "I sure walked into a trap."

"No talk," Donal warned. "I'm in a killing mood, Gober."

The bedroom door opened. Ruth came quickly into the office. Her eyes were bright, her cheeks pink with excitement.

Gober gaped at her stupidly. He seemed like a man in a trance. Donal prodded him with the gun.

"We're putting you back to bed," he said. "We'll tuck you in with your boss, Gober."

The gangling foreman stumbled into the bedroom, hands held above his head. Donal nodded to the girl. She pressed the long barrel of the .45 against his back.

Donal holstered his own gun. "Don't hesitate," he said to her. "If he tries to move—shoot."

"I ain't movin'," Gober whispered, hoarsely. His fascinated gaze was on the man under the blankets. He could see Jasey's eyes, wild, glaring. Gober spoke again, in the same hoarse whisper. "I warned you, Anse . . . I warned you plenty that Cameron would get you for this gal bus'ness."

Donal picked up the remains of the hair rope. "I've changed my mind about putting you to bed." He threw Jasey a derisive grin. "You and your boss might get to fighting too much." He eyed a heavy chair that stood near one of the windows. He knew that chair. Old Jim Daker had had it made from native oak brought down from the hills. It was a massive piece of furniture, a good load for two strong men.

Obeying Donal's gesture, Gober lowered himself into the chair. Donal tied his hands to the side posts and secured his ankles firmly to the chair legs. He wound what was left of the rope about his middle and knotted the ends to the chair-back.

Ruth brought him a strip she tore from the window curtain. Donal dangled the piece of cloth in his hand, stared with implacable eyes at the glowering death's-head face. "Where's Alamo?" He touched the man's head significantly with the barrel of his gun. "Don't want to crack your skull for you."

"He ain't fur—" Gober was breathing noisily. "Same place we throwed you into the mornin' we jumped you on the trail."

"Torres with him?"

Gober nodded, apprehensive eyes on the gun.

"How many men on guard?"

"One, I reckon—"

"Where's Ferrel?"

"Snorin' his head off."

Donal wasted no more time with further questions. He drew Gober's head back, forced in the gag and knotted the ends.

He gave the girl a satisfied nod and they both hurried back to the office, Donal pausing to close and lock the bedroom door. He pocketed the key.

Ruth looked at him intently, questioningly. She knew the purpose in his mind.

"It's going to be dangerous," she said.

"It can be done." His eyes were steely points, bright with determination. "I'm wondering what to do with you?"

"I'm going with you," Ruth said. She smiled faintly. "I feel safer with you, no matter where you go."

He gave her a grin, seemed still hesitant, his eyes troubled, perplexed. "You can't go . . . no chance."

She slipped a hand through his arm, leaned close to him. "Where you go, I go, always, from now on." Her voice was low, hardly more than a whisper.

He went pale, but she saw by his eyes that his decision was final. She said, faintly, "All right. I won't interfere."

Donal drew her close, an arm around her waist. "Listen—I've got to pull off a trick . . . that's why we can't chance anybody seeing you with me."

"A trick?" She liked the feel of his arm. There was strength in it, and tenderness.

"I've got to fool the man on guard at the granary," Donal continued. "The only way is to head toward him from the bunkhouse. He has no reason to suspect that anything is wrong. It's dark . . . he'll think I'm one of the outfit." He grinned down at her. "I fooled the man at your door the same way."

"Couldn't I hide somewhere, not too far from you? Those chinaberry trees—near the corral."

Donal assented with a feeling of relief. She would be safer out there than left in the house alone. There was just a chance somebody else would be wondering about those two sharp clangs from the bell.

They left the room by way of the veranda door and plunged into the grove of trees. The moon was up, Donal discovered with some misgiving.

He led the girl stealthily around the high patio wall, and on past the tankhouse. From there on they kept to the cover of the bushes. Shep padded quietly at their heels.

Moonlight lay like snowdrift in the big yard on the other side of the fence. No life stirred there—only loud, reassuring snores from the bunkhouse, now in darkness.

They reached the cluster of chinaberry trees. The shadows were deep under their thick spread of branches. Satisfied the girl was practically invisible except to closely-searching eyes, Donal worked his way back along the fence and entered the yard from behind the bunkhouse.

Ruth's gaze followed him anxiously. He had been lucky, so far. She frowned. It wasn't luck that got him into the house, enabled him to overpower three men single-handed. She had seen his cool, efficient brain at work. He thought things out, planned every move. He was swift, courageous, action personified. The very boldness of his plan to rescue Alamo and Torres would carry him to success.

She watched, every nerve taut, glimpsed his tall form drifting up the yard. His hat was pulled over his face. He looked just like any other cowboy on his reluctant way to relieve a fellow-member of the outfit from a boring, wearisome task.

The guard lifted his head in a casual glance at the dark figure approaching through the moonlight. He got up from the box on which he leaned against the adobe wall of the granary, yawned, and fished a tobacco sack from his shirt pocket. He had no reason to suspect anything wrong. Gober had promised to send a man to relieve him when the moon showed over the mountains. The long wait had not improved his temper.

"Damn long time gittin' here," he complained. "I'm sure fed up with playin' watch-dog." He spilled yellow flakes into thin brown cigarette paper, lowered eyes intent on the operation.

Perhaps the newcomer's continued silence made him suspicious. He looked up, muttered a shocked ejaculation, stared with horrified eyes at the gun menacing him. Paper and tobacco slipped from his fingers, and obeying Donal's gesture he slowly lifted his hands over his head.

Donal relieved him of the gun that sagged in holster. He gestured again, at the heavy, fortress-like door in the adobe wall.

The man understood, obediently walked in front of him to the door, turned the key and gave the door a push.

Donal followed him into the yawning darkness of the granary, reached out a hand to give the door a closing shove. The momentary inattention gave the man his chance. He was tough-minded, cool and fast. He sprang aside, whirled like a cat, grabbed Donal's wrist and forced the gun down. His free arm coiled around Donal's neck in a choking grip.

The door finished its swing, clicked shut. The two men struggled in a tomb-like blackness touched only by faint rectangles of moon glow from the small windows set high in the walls.

The man was a grizzly bear for strength. The powerful hand on Donal's wrist tightened its hold, fingers fastened over the gun.

Donal wrenched his hand free and swung a crushing blow. The man groaned, his clutching arm slipped from Donal's neck.

Donal sidestepped, swung the heavy gun-barrel again. The man collapsed, sprawled senseless at his feet.

The savage encounter had taken Donal's wind. He stood motionless, breathing hard. Something stirred in the darkness—the rustle of straw.

Donal said, in a low whisper, *"Alamo—"*

A strangled grunt answered him.

Donal bent over the man lying at his feet. He was not dead, but the life in him was very feeble. There would be no more trouble from him for a long time.

Satisfied, Donal felt his way through the darkness, guided by grunts from Alamo. His fumbling fingers found and unfastened the gag from the old man's mouth, went swiftly to work on the cords knotted around wrists and ankles.

Alamo sat up, spat slobber from sore lips. "Son," he croaked, " 'minds me of the time your dad got me loose from Lobo Jack's bunch of killers. You sure got his fightin' guts in you."

He rubbed numbed wrists and legs. "Whar's the gal?"

Donal reassured him, handed over the gun he had taken from the senseless guard. "Tie that man up while I get Torres loose," he said. He put the cords into Alamo's hand.

"Cain't see whar the skunk lays in this dark," Alamo said.

"Move straight ahead. You'll fall over him."

Donal crawled on along the wall toward the sound made by feet kicking on straw.

In something like two minutes he had the Mexican free of his bonds and was guiding him to the door where they found Alamo working on the unconscious man.

"No sense, tyin' his mouth up," the mountain man whispered. "This hombre won't wake up for mebbe a couple of hours."

Donal opened the door cautiously and took a look into the moonlit yard. No sound broke the stillness. He said, "All right . . . let's go—"

They were outside. Donal turned the key in the heavy padlock, put the key in his pocket and moved swiftly toward the fence. He was in desperate haste to get back to the girl he had left waiting under the chinaberry tree. She would be anxious. He wanted to end her suspense.

Nobody spoke, feet made no sound, they drifted like shadows across that wide expanse of revealing moonlight.

They reached the fence. Alamo said, softly, "Somebody comin', Don . . . ridin' like hell up the avenue."

"I've been listening—" Donal spoke worriedly. "We must get Ruth away from here, fast." He told them about the two horses cached across the creek.

Alamo nodded contentedly. "You an' the gal git movin'," he urged. "Pasqual an' me will grab us a couple of broncs." He glanced at the corral. "Reckon we'll sneak out a couple right now. Huh, Pasqual?"

"*Si*—" The Mexican hesitated and he gave Donal a curious look.

"No time for palaver," Alamo grumbled. "Let's grab us them broncs, an' a couple of saddles. Thar's hell due to pop when that hombre gits here."

Others had heard the rapidly-approaching hoofbeats. Lamplight sprang out from the bunk-house windows. Men were astir in there.

Donal grabbed at the fence rail. Alamo was right. Trouble was heading into the yard. He must get Ruth across the creek before it was too late. It was only a matter of minutes before Jasey and Gober were discovered in the locked bedroom.

He swung over the fence. Pasqual's voice again stopped him.

"Señor"—Pasqual peered at him between the fence rails—"you must listen. It is important—"

The gravity in his voice held them rigid, heedless of the growing uproar lower down in the yard where a lone rider slid from his saddle and lurched unsteadily toward the men who streamed noisily from the bunkhouse. He collapsed.

"Señor . . . Anse Jasey is *Salvador Antista*—"

22

Pasqual's amazing revelation was like a revealing flare of lightning. In one brief, comprehending moment the jumbled pieces of the puzzle fell into their proper places, made the picture complete. Anson Jasey, as he called himself, was Salvador Antista in whose veins ran the proud blood of the Salazars, one-time lords of the vast Rio Seco, by royal grant from a king of Spain.

Pasqual had more to tell him. Pedro Cordero, a newcomer from Mexico City, had recognized Antista, who in turn realized that his secret was in danger. He knew that Pedro had talked to Pasqual and took steps to silence them.

"He murdered my friend, señor—"

Alamo nodded. "I cut him down from the tree, laid him in the cabin—"

"*Gracias.*" Pasqual spoke gratefully. "Pedro was a good hombre."

"Why didn't they hang *you?*" Donal asked.

"Antista had big ideas, señor. He wanted to use me, told me that if I worked with him he would make me *El Señor Administrador.*"

Pasqual's story had stripped the mantle of mystery from the man, laid bare the secret ambition of this scheming and ruthless marauder.

The years will roll back . . . I will come into my own.

Boastful words that revealed the motive that had driven Jasey to pillage and murder—to insanity.

He heard Ruth's low voice: "Donal—I couldn't wait any longer. I saw you come over the fence. Donal—what's happening?"

He gestured for silence. "Listen—"

The sound that drifted on the night wind was like low, muttering thunder, the drumming hoofs of horses on the dead run.

They heard a man's frantic shout. "Ain't stickin' round to trade lead with that Circle C bunch!"

In an instant the group of men scattered like wind-driven leaves. Dust spurted from bootheels as they fled in panic toward the barn.

Two men remained by the prone body of the rider who had brought the news. Donal recognized Ferrel's strident and bitter voice. "Looks like he's bleedin' to death!"

"Hell!" yelled the other man. "Leave him lay. I'm gittin' away from here pronto." He broke into a run for the barn.

Red flame spurted from behind him and as the sharp crack of the gun touched their ears the fascinated watchers saw the running man go down as if struck by a bolt of lightning.

Donal heard Ruth's shocked whisper. "He's killed Squint!"

Smoking gun in hand, Ferrel ran toward the

house. They heard the slam of the kitchen door, his voice, yelling for Gober.

The rataplan of hoofs drew up the avenue. Circle C's fighting outfit was coming on the jump. Donal's heart leaped.

Ruth saw and understood the bleak look in his eyes. Her hand fastened on his arm. "No!" She spoke frantically. "Let them go! You've done enough!"

He stood irresolute. Yells and curses came from the barn where frightened men were hastily throwing on saddles. Riders streamed from the wide door and galloped furiously in the direction of the creek, to the safety of the hills. Those lucky enough to shake off pursuit would eventually escape across the border.

Donal was not caring much about these men. They were the small fry. Sooner or later the law would catch up with them, or they would die violently at the hands of some ruthless fellow-killer.

He had different and very definite ideas about Jasey and Gober. He knew now that Squint was the actual murderer of Rusty Cross, but it was Jasey and Gober who had planned the crime. He wanted them to hang according to the law of the land, and he wanted Ben Ferrel to hang. There was a dead man lying in a lonely cabin and Ferrel had murdered him. Also there was another reason why these men should be brought to justice.

"They murdered your father," he said to Ruth. "We must not let them escape."

She had no answer for him.

He took the heavy .45 dangling in her hand and thrust it at Pasqual. "You and Alamo look out for her." He was suddenly running along the fence, toward the house.

Ruth looked at Alamo piteously. The old mountain man gave her a grim, understanding nod.

"Don't you git to worryin'," he said, gently. "I'll jest trail along with him."

Ruth watched him go, deep fear in her eyes, and gratitude. She felt Pasqual's look, grave, understanding, but quietly confident.

"Do not fear, señorita. God walks with him, as He walked with the old señor."

She smiled at him for that, said, impulsively, "God surely walked with *you,* Pasqual."

"*Si*!" He spoke feelingly. "I had not hoped to be alive, when the sun lifts this morning." Excitement deepened his voice. "Señorita—our men—they come fast. See—it is old Bearcat—and Brasca who ride with them. *Por Dios*! They carry death in their hands!"

Horsemen poured into the big ranch yard. Ruth heard the wild yipping yell of Circle C on the warpath, the crackle of gunfire as some half dozen of the cornered men spurred from the barn in a desperate attempt to escape across the creek.

Pasqual pulled the girl down behind a barricade of piled fence posts. She lay there, quivering with excitement and fears, terrorizing fears for the man she loved. Shep cuddled close, licked her hand.

Ferrel knew nothing of Donal's earlier activities, but Gober's disappearance, the muffled groans behind the locked bedroom door, told him that strange things had been happening while he snored in the bunkhouse.

Muttering imprecations, he forced the lock and ran into the room. He took one aghast look and hastily reached for his jackknife.

He worked swiftly and in less than a minute Gober was on his feet. He watched stupidly while his friend cut Jasey loose.

"What the hell's goin' on outside?" he asked. He cocked his head, listened attentively to the nearing thunder of hoofs.

"Circle C's on the prod," Ferrel answered. "Our bunch has quit us cold . . . ain't got the guts to stand up to Circle C—damn their yeller hides."

"Squint? He gone, too?"

"He figgered to," snarled Ferrel. "He didn't git fur. I blowed his light out. The damn half-breed had it comin'."

He helped Jasey from the bed and ran to one of the windows, peered cautiously into the moonlit grove. Gober joined him and together they watched the whirlwind approach of the men from Circle C.

"Soon as they git into the yard we'll hightail it through them trees and head for the Lobo Canyon camp," Ferrel muttered. "We can git broncs there and light out for the border."

"A hell of a long walk," growled Gober. He rubbed aching muscles.

Ferrel looked at him curiously. "How come you and the boss got hawg-tied?"

"Don Cameron," grunted the lanky foreman. He gave the other man his ghastly grin.

Ferrel swore softly. "Told you all along we should have set that hombre dancin' on air when we nabbed him on the trail."

The last of the riders vanished into the yard. Dust drifted through the trees.

Ferrel put a leg over the window-sill, glanced back at Jasey, still motionless by the bed. He seemed like a man in a trance.

"Comin', boss?" Ferrel's whisper was a hoarse rasp that brought Jasey's head round in a dazed look at him. "Now's our chance to git through the trees," Ferrel urged.

He dropped from the window, stood outside, still looking in at Jasey.

Gober shook his head gloomily. "He's gone loco." His big hand groped at his thigh and for the first time he seemed to realize that no heavy holster sagged there. Dismay spread over his face. “Ain’t even got my shirt,” he groaned; and without another glance at the stony-faced man by the bed, he slid through the window.

Donal was in the hall when he heard the shot. He came to an abrupt standstill, was conscious of a drawling voice behind him.

“Sounds like a derringer—” Alamo loomed out of the darkness. “Sure was a derringer, son—”

Donal glared. “I told you to stay with Ruth—”

Alamo let out a low chuckle. “You ain’t my boss, young feller. I left my boss out thar with Pasqual. Ain’t for me to set back when she tells me to stick close to you.”

Thundering hoofs surged past the house, and above the crackling gunfire they heard the shrill yips of Circle C’s fighting men.

Donal grinned at the gaunt old mountain man. “Bearcat,” he said softly, “and old Brasca. It’s the showdown, Alamo!” He went swiftly into the empty office where the lamp still glowed on the table.

The bedroom door stood open. It was dark in there, and very still.

Alamo said, softly, “Careful, son—” He jerked the lamp-chain, snuffed out the light.

They moved stealthily through the darkness and came to the open doorway. They halted again, ears keyed for any betraying sound. From where he stood, Donal could see the big chair, faintly touched by moonlight from the window behind. Gober was gone, which meant that Ferrel had been one jump ahead of them.

Something stirred in there. They heard a low moan of pain, a strangled gasp.

Donal suddenly understood. He pushed into the room and bent over the man lying on the floor. "Jasey," he said over his shoulder to Alamo. "Shot himself."

Alamo put a match to the lamp on a table near the bed, stooped and picked up the small gun lying under Jasey's hand. "Said it was a derringer," he drawled. He tossed the ugly little weapon on the tumbled bed. "Kilt hisself, huh?"

"He's still breathing—"

A man shouted from somewhere in the cottonwood grove, and they heard the crashing report of a .45—another shout, and then stillness again.

The man gasping on the floor opened glazing eyes that stared up at them with the ferocity of a dying wolf.

"Salvador Antista will not live to hang like a common felon." His voice was surprisingly strong. "I am Antista, last of the Salazar blood. This country of the Rio Seco is mine by right of birth, Cameron. With my last breath I lay claim to Circle C, to Rocking D, and all the land within a hundred leagues." He shuddered, was suddenly silent.

"Crazy as a loon," muttered Alamo.

"He's dead," Donal told him. He stood up.

"I'm not sorry. The man was mad—insane."

"A damn murderer." Alamo's eyes were hard. "A killin' skunk."

Footsteps clattered into the hall, the quick scrape and jangle of spurs, Bearcat's loud, demanding voice.

They crowded into the room, grim-faced men, smelling of dust and sweat of battle.

"Dead, huh?"

Bearcat gazed with bitter eyes at the still form.

"Shot himself," Donal informed them.

"Figgered to git Jasey my own self," growled Brasca.

"His real name is Salvador Antista," Donal said.

There was a stunned silence, broken by Donal.

"How come you boys got here so handy?" he wanted to know.

Bearcat came out of his trance. "Waal, Don, your ma got to figgerin' you'd mebbe need us. We couldn't find no track of the gal and when we got back to the ranch she said for us to burn dust gittin' over to Rockin' D."

"We sure burned dust," chuckled Brasca. "Got here in time to grab us most a dozen of Gober's wolves."

"Got Gober, too," Bearcat said in a satisfied voice. "Nabbed him makin' a sneak through the cottonwoods. Had no gun on him."

"Got Ferrel, too," added Brasca, contentedly.

"He acted tough and Scarface killed him first shot."

"Reckon that was the shot we heerd out in the cottonwoods," commented Alamo.

"Sure was," chuckled Bearcat. "Picked up Squint, layin' out in the yard. Bullet nicked his spine, but I reckon he'll live to swing."

"He killed Rusty Cross," Donal said, and his eyes were hard.

"We got more news for you," Bearcat continued. "It was Bittner killed the gal's dad. The feller we grabbed at Sheep Springs spilled the story." Bearcat paused, glanced uncertainly at Ruth and Pasqual hurrying in from the hall.

"She has a right to know the truth," Donal told him. He drew the girl to his side, clasped her hand.

"Waal, seems like the colonel sent for Bittner, figgerin' he was sheriff, and let on he had evidence that would put Gober and Ferrel behind the bars for stealin' Rockin' D cows. Bittner jest natcherally passed on the word to Jasey"—Bearcat paused, glanced at the dead man—"Antista, I mean, and Antista fixed for Bittner to go out to the ranch, pertendin' he was all set to arrest Gober and Ferrel. The colonel rode out to the crik with him, whar Gober and Ferrel was planted all set for the killin'. Bittner tells the colonel to git down from his horse and help him git the handcuffs on and when the colonel's back was turned he knocked him senseless with his gun." Bearcat gave Ruth a worried look. "Hate to be tellin' you," he added unhappily. "Reckon you savvy the rest of it."

Ruth was glad of the firm hand clasping her own. She said, simply, "I wanted the truth, Bearcat." Her wet eyes lifted to Donal. "I—I'd like to go—"

Donal's look went questioningly to Alamo. The old mountain man nodded. "We'll take care of things here, son. You git Ruthie over to them horses you got cached acrost the crik."

The trail climbed through piñons and junipers and sprawling oaks, and the moon rode with them.

They would rest in the meadows, Donal decided, in the high, green meadows under the whispering pines. He would tell her about the eagles, about his father, and Rusty's bear.

He would tell her a lot of things.

Center Point Large Print
600 Brooks Road / PO Box 1
Thorndike, ME 04986-0001 USA

(207) 568-3717

US & Canada:
1 800 929-9108
www.centerpointlargeprint.com